MICHELLE LYNN ROSS

Single In A Small Town

Madison and Bryan

To anyone starting over and learning to love yourself again.

Acknowledgments

This book wouldn't exist without the people who keep showing up for me.

To my readers: Thank you for continuing to come back to Fawn Creek. Your support means the world to me. Every message, review, recommendation and social media post keeps this dream going and I'm so grateful for you.

To my kids: Thank you for being patient with me when I get lost in my fictional world and get dinner on the table late so I can finish up one more scene.

To my husband: Thank you for believing in me and for cheering me on when I want to throw my laptop in the trash. Also, thank you for supporting our family so I can chase my dreams of being a writer. I love you. My life wouldn't be the same without you.

Also, shout out to Dala for being my ARC reader for this story. I appreciate your help so much!

Chapter 1

"Shit! Shit, shit, shit!" I stammer as I jump from the bed, wrapping the flat sheet around my naked body as my feet land on the floor.

Bryan startles at the sound of my voice, also springing up from the bed, using a pillow to cover his manhood. He surveys the room, looking for the source of my panic before looking back at me. "What is your problem? I thought an iguana had climbed into the bed with us or something. You almost gave me a heart attack."

"You! Us!" I shriek, waving my hands around the room. "This is my problem." I groan. "Your sister is going to kill me. I can't believe this. What have we done?"

Bryan shakes his head, still obviously confused. "I... I don't understand. Why is she going to kill you? Were you supposed to meet her this morning or something?"

I let out a heavy sigh. "No." My heart is still pounding in my chest.

"Then why is she going to kill you? I don't get it. What am I missing?"

I shake my head and move around the room, gathering my dress and undergarments from where they were tossed around the room the night before. Then I make my way towards the bathroom door before turning to look back at him. "Because Bryan, she is not only one of my daycare clients, but she is my friend! She invited me to come on this trip to be a part of her wedding, not to sleep with her brother." With that, I disappear into the bathroom to get dressed.

When I step back into the room, Bryan is sitting on the edge of the bed, now wearing his boxers. He grins as our eyes meet. He still doesn't get it. "So, basically it was a two-for-one special.... A wedding and some fantastic sex... if I do say so myself." He smiles smugly. "What more could you ask for?"

I turn and face the full-length mirror next to the bathroom door, finger combing my blonde hair into a messy ponytail. "It's really not that funny. Now I have to do the walk of shame across the resort in my bridesmaid dress. What if someone sees me? How am I going to explain this?" I ask, motioning to my reflection.

"Want me to lend you some clothes?" Bryan teases. "I mean, they might be a little big, but you wouldn't be wearing your dress from last night."

I, however, don't think Bryan is funny. I roll my eyes and turn to face Bryan head on, trying to fight back my tears. His face softens as he sees my haggard expression.

"Hey." He says, moving towards me and wrapping me into a tight hug against his chest. "It's okay. Avery will not be mad at you, and if she is, blame it on me. I have zero regrets about what we did last night, Madison, and you shouldn't either. We are both grown, consenting adults on vacation in paradise. We scratched an itch that obviously both of us needed scratched. No harm, no foul."

I let out a heavy sigh into his chest before leaning my head back to look at him. "Okay, but seriously. Avery can not know about this. Promise me. I don't want this to cause any problems with our friendship, and I really don't want it to cause issues with my business."

Bryan holds his pinkie into the air. "Pinkie promise." He declares. "Our secret is safe with me."

I step back, creating some space between us before hooking my pinkie into his. "Deal." I grumble.

"You sure you don't want to do that one more time before you go?" He asks, wiggling his eyebrows. "I won't tell if you don't."

I widen my eyes and glare at him. "Bryan." I hiss. "That can't happen again and it won't. You were right. We were both drinking last night and got carried away. But that's all. Now, if you'll excuse me, I have to sneak to my room without getting caught by our friends." I pause, letting every worse case scenario flood into my brain. "Oh my gosh, what if your mom sees me? She'll know. Mom's always know."

He lets out a heavy sigh and sits back down on his bed in a huff. "Stop stressing. I bet no one will even be up yet. Hell, with the way they were drinking at the nightclub, I'm willing to bet no one else will even be up until noon today. And knowing my mom, she is having room service breakfast in her room with Juliet."

"I hope you're right." I mumble, placing my hand on the doorknob.

Slowly, I turn the handle and open the door just enough to allow me to peek into the hallway. Much to my surprise and approval, the hall is quiet and empty, with only the sounds of shuffling coming from the housekeeping staff downstairs. I turn back to face Bryan once more. "The coast is clear. I'm going to make a mad dash for my room."

He shrugs. "If you insist. See you later, Freckles."

I scowl and close the door once more, turning back to face him. "What did you just call me?"

"Freckles." He repeats. When I don't reply, he continues. "The sun down here has really brought out the freckles across your nose and made them pop. I like them. I didn't notice them when I first met you, but now I can't get enough of them." He confesses.

I shake my head. "That's because I go to great lengths to cover them up. I've always hated them. In fact, I used to beg for my parents to get me something to get rid of them when I was a kid." I admit. "Besides, you and I are not close enough to be on a nickname basis."

He raises a brow and a sly smile spreads across his face. "Based on the sounds you were making last night, I beg to differ."

I let out an exasperated huff. "Okay, on that note, I'm leaving. See you later."

"Bye." He replies with a grin, as I reopen the door and slip into the hall.

Carrying my sandals from the night before, and of course, wearing my satin bridesmaid's dress, I scurry down the hall, key card in hand. As soon as I reach my room, I insert my key and bolt inside, closing the door behind me. Relief rushes over me as I rest against the wooden door. I made it.

I can take a shower and relax in my room and put my terrible decision from last night behind me. Until a knock at the door foils my plan.

Damnit.

I spin and stand on tiptoe to check the peephole. My friend, Sierra, is standing in the hall, arms crossed in front of her chest as she waits impatiently.

"Um, hang on just a second!" I call out to her as my eyes dart frantically around the room. Thinking quickly, I grab the white robe that's hanging on a hook outside the bathroom door and put it on over my dress. But, when I turn to check my reflection, I remember the robe is only knee length. My satin dress is longer than the robe itself, and is blowing my cover.

Quickly, I untie the robe once again and work to gather the hem of my floor-length skirt before bunching it up at my waist. I bind the string and check the mirror one last time. Satisfied that I'm covered, in more ways than one, I reach over to open the door. I just have to get rid of Sierra, then I'm home free. If she didn't see me come into my room in the first place, that is.

"About time you answered." She says, pushing her way into the room. "Were you still sleeping?" She's wearing a baseball cap and black swim cover with a pair of flip-flops. You can see the outline of her bright blue bikini under the sheer fabric. Her red hair falls over her shoulders in her signature springy curls.

I look at her and then back to my perfectly made bed that obviously wasn't slept in last night.

Shit. I'm obviously busted.

"I just got up a little bit ago and was doing some tidying up." I lie.

Sierra raises one brow at me. "Well, that's enough playing maid. You're on vacation. The housekeepers will make the bed for you, you know?" She says, rolling her eyes. "Put on your swimsuit and come down to the pool with me. We have a full day of poolside day drinking ahead of us."

After last night, and too many mixed drinks following the wedding, the mere thought of alcohol touching my lips makes me want to vomit. Memories of Bryan and I on the dance floor

5

in the nightclub last night race into my brain. When it all went downhill.

I can't do that again today. "Sierra, I don't know. I'm still pretty tired from last night."

"Nonsense." She interrupts, holding up a finger in front of my face to stop me. "This is our last day in Mexico, and I refuse to let you sleep it away. I already have a row of chairs saved around the pool. You can't make me sit down there by myself like a loser."

I resist. "I'm just kind of worn out from last night."

Sierra rolls her eyes. She obviously won't take no for an answer. "You can rest by the water. They'll even bring you breakfast if you tip well enough. Let's go."

"But..." I pause, searching for another excuse. "I should really work on packing. I have stuff all over this room."

Sierra is losing her patience, and there is an obvious tone of annoyance in her voice. "You can pack later. Come on, let's go and enjoy the weather. Do you know it's snowing back home? You can't let a poolside day in January go to waste. I won't allow it."

She is really not going to let me out of this. Suddenly, I feel my satin bridesmaid dress breaking free from the bunched knot under the tie of the robe. I'm going to get busted. There's no doubt about it. Then I'll have some real explaining to do. I have to act quickly.

"Okay, fine." I agree. "Just let me take a quick shower and I'll meet you down there. I promise. No more than fifteen minutes."

Sierra rolls her eyes, but she nods in acceptance. "Fine. fifteen minutes. But if you are one minute late, I'll call the front desk to do a welfare check on you. Don't test me. I'll embarrass the shit out of you. And I won't lose a wink of sleep over it."

I open the door and gesture for her to move into the hall. "Oh believe me, I know." I say with a chuckle. "I'll be down in a few."

Reluctantly, Sierra leaves the room, eyeing me suspiciously. I close the door and let out a deep breath. The coast is clear and no one will ever know what Bryan and I did last night. What happens in paradise, stays in paradise. Right?

Chapter 2

Within twelve minutes, I'm making my way towards the row of seats Sierra has saved for our crew, each marked with a resort beach towel. Sierra is laying in a chair right in the middle, staring at her watch when I approach her.

"That was close. I was just getting ready to call the front desk." She teases as I take a seat next to her with two iced coffees in hand. "You even had time to stop at the cafe. Impressive." She adds, accepting her drink from my outstretched hand. "Thank you."

"You're welcome." I respond, as I kick off my sandals and settle into the chair next to her. "Thanks for making me come down here against my will. I would definitely regret missing out on this. Is it really snowing at home? Or did you just say that to make me feel bad?"

Sierra groans. "Yes. My weather alerts would not stop going off last night. Cody is watching the security cameras like a hawk because he's worried sick about his cows. I told him they are cows, they will be fine, but he is seriously obsessed. He wouldn't even leave the room because he's worried about losing Wi-Fi."

I frown. "Are they okay? I know nothing about taking care of cows."

"Honestly, I have no idea. But, they have fur, so, probably?" She says with a shrug. "Surely, they aren't the first cows to be out in the snow."

"They're fine." Cody grumbles, interrupting our conversation as he makes his way around the row of chairs and settles in on the other side of Sierra. "Nathan is going to run by and make sure there's enough hay and that they can get into the barn."

Nathan is my little brother. He works part time for Cody and Andrew during the warmer months hauling hay and helping with the cattle.

"Good. Now you can enjoy the last day of our trip." Sierra smirks.

I pick up my phone and open the Facebook app. Absentmindedly, I scroll to Ben's profile just as Sierra leans over to see what I'm doing.

"Ew, get off his page." She commands. "He is your exhusband and he doesn't deserve any of your attention while you're on vacation. I don't care that your divorce was just finalized."

"I just want to see if he's posted any photos of the girls playing in the snow. I miss them and I feel like I haven't seen them in ages. I can barely remember what they look like." I say, waving her off as I continue to scroll down on his page. There aren't any new photos, but what I see in his feed stops me in my tracks and causes my stomach to turn. I should have never looked at his profile.

Sierra notices the change in my expression immediately. "What's wrong? What'd he do now?"

I turn the phone to show her that Ben has recently updated his relationship status.

9

In a relationship with Amber Calloway.

Sierra groans. "Is that her? The one he had the affair with?" She asks, taking my phone from my hand and clicking on the woman's profile picture.

I nod. "You know it."

"Gross. She even looks like a home wrecking whore." Sierra says, scrunching her face. "Well, he definitely traded down with that one. You are so much better off without him, and eventually you'll be counting your blessings that you got away from him. Now put your phone away and enjoy the last of this trip before you have to go back to Kansas and deal with his ugly ass."

I scoff. "He's not that ugly." I say, trying to defend him. "I was with that guy for a long time, you know. At one point, I loved him and thought he was the hottest guy to walk the Earth."

"Well, turns out he's ugly on the inside and that's all that really matters." She shrugs. "He could rush into a burning building to save a dozen kittens and I'd still hate him. I'll never forgive him for what he put you through. I have major bitch eating cracker syndrome with him now."

I furrow my brow. "What's bitch eating cracker syndrome?"

Sierra sits up slightly before turning towards me. "You've seriously never heard of bitch eating cracker syndrome? It's when you dislike someone so much that every single thing they do gets on your nerves. For example, they could just be minding their own business, eating a snack, but it's still annoying because of who they are. So, you might say, 'Just look at that bitch over there eating crackers like they own the place.'"

I laugh and shake my head. "I have never heard of that."

"Well, now you'll use it all the time. So, you're welcome." She laughs.

"I bet you're right." I admit before turning my attention back to my phone and the mess in front of me. This isn't fair. I was putting off changing my relationship status for as long as I could. Not because I wanted to save our marriage, or because I thought we might get back together. Only because I knew once it was changed, the questions and the rumors would flood through our small town of Fawn Creek, Kansas.

Now, I guess the wait is over. I have no other choice but to accept it. I scroll to my page and pause. My status has automatically defaulted to "in a relationship" but with no name next to the status, because of Ben changing his own. I frown and make the updates, changing my own to single.

Single.

I haven't been single since I was in junior high.

Hell, I haven't been single for as long as I've had Facebook.

Now, here it is, loud and clear. Suddenly, my business is everyone's business, and the people waiting back home will definitely remind me of this. Suddenly, I'm not looking forward to going back home tomorrow.

Sierra leans over and squeezes my hand in silence.

This is harder than I thought it would be. Sometimes I still think I'm going to wake up and find out it was all a bad dream. However, I just keep waking up to the same crazy reality.

It wasn't long ago that Ben was assuring me that this Amber girl was crazy and lying about their relationship. He would never have an affair, he promised. She was just trying to make him lose his job. She meant nothing to him. Too bad his cell phone records proved differently.

While checking through our phone bills, I found months and

11

months' worth of phone calls and text messages exchanged between Ben and a number that turned out to belong to Amber. That was the night I knew I had to end it.

Even as I served him divorce papers, he denied that the entire thing ever took place. How could I have been so stupid for so long?

"It's okay, friend. This needed to happen. And you can't move on without pulling the plug." Sierra says, still with her hand resting on mine. Almost as though she is going through all of my emotions with me.

I frown. She's right, of course. The divorce is final. We haven't lived together since before Thanksgiving. It's not like we were going to get back together. It just hasn't been easy. Ben and I had been together since junior high. He was my first love, my first actual boyfriend, and basically my entire life for as long as I can remember. It's still hard to imagine a future without him in it.

I take one last look at the change to my profile and then tuck my phone away. "Okay, it's Facebook official. Now I can only hope that the Fawn Creek busy bodies won't blow up my inbox at least until I get home. I just want to enjoy this last bit of vacation that I have left." I say, watching Bryan round the corner with a cup of coffee in his hand as he makes his way towards our group. Seeing him with his T-shirt draped over his shoulder and his exposed chest causes memories to rush back from last night. Heat floods to my cheeks.

Bryan isn't the typical type of guy that women tend to fawn over and certainly not my idea of a dream guy. While I wouldn't consider him out of shape by any means, he's not ripped and muscular like the guys from the romance novels I see gracing the covers at Tyler's bookstore. His body is a little bigger and much softer. Husky. More of a teddy bear than a Chippendale dancer. I can't explain it, but I admit, I like it. Laying my head on his chest last night was comfortable. Soft, secure, safe. Something I could do again.

Well, I mean, if he wasn't my best friend's brother. And if he didn't live 5 hours away and if I wasn't freshly divorced and in the middle of rebuilding my life. Who am I kidding? Five seconds ago, I was heartbroken over my ex-husband. I'm not ready to move on. And when I do become ready, it can't be with Bryan.

Bryan takes a seat in the chair next to Cody after offering me a soft smile.

Instantly, thoughts of the two of us tangled in his bed sheets last night come back to me. I shake my head, almost as though I'm trying to clear my thoughts.

Stop it.

"Good. Now what you need is a one-night stand." Sierra decides, adding to a conversation that I forgot we were even having. "Just something meaningless to officially start your single life off on the right foot."

"I don't think that's a good idea." I say, shaking my head. Immediately, I can feel the blood rushing to my face once again.

"Yep, it is." Sierra argues. "Madison, you've slept with one man over the course of your entire life. I don't know Ben well, but from looking at him, I have to guess that your sex life has been pretty disappointing so far. Seriously, you need to get out there and find out what an actual orgasm feels like. You need just one good banging to really reset your love life. There's more to life than missionary, you know."

Bryan interrupts the moment by choking on his coffee. My eyes dart to his to send him a "don't you dare" kind of glare.

13

Sierra raises a brow and glances between the two of us but doesn't say a word.

"Let's go to the club tonight." Sierra suggests. "What could be better than a one-night stand in Mexico with a man you'll never see again? Want to join us, Bryan?" She asks, turning towards him.

"Nah, thanks for the invite, Sierra, but I think I'm going to sit this one out. I learned my lesson last night at that club. Rubbing elbows with literally everyone in the resort was too much for me. I need a break from all peoply activities before I go back home and back to work."

"Not a fan of crowds, I take it?" Sierra asks.

"Not even a little. I'm sure the military didn't help, but something about being surrounded by people just puts me on high alert. Especially people I don't know and trust. As fun as this has been, I am ready to get back home and have a little bit of peace and quiet. You have fun tonight, though." He says, now with his eyes on me.

I pause, my eyes bouncing from Sierra to Bryan. "Actually, I'm planning to stay in, too." I admit. "This week has kicked my butt."

"Madison, you have to go out." Sierra argues. "This is your chance!"

"No, I really can't. I'm exhausted already and when we get back home tomorrow evening, it's back to reality. No midday naps or relaxing in the bathtub while I read a book. I'm going to take advantage of my downtime the best I can."

Sierra shakes her head. "Whatever, party pooper. I'll let you off the hook this time, but this isn't over."

Chapter 3

I clutch my beach bag over my shoulder and make my way into the resort. After a full morning of hanging out in the sun, followed by lunch, Sierra has finally set me free. So, I'm headed to my room for a shower and to pack my things for our trip home tomorrow. But first, coffee.

I step into the resort cafe and order a caramel macchiato. While standing in line, waiting for my drink, I'm ambushed by one of my favorite tiny humans running up to hug my leg.

"Madi!" Juliet squeals as she wraps her arms around my leg.

I smile and bend down to scoop up Juliet, as Bryan makes his way towards us.

"Hi sweet girl. Are you hanging out with your Uncle Bryan?"

Juliet's head nods quickly as she looks back at her uncle with a grin. "That's my Bryan."

"Yeah it is. Are you having fun?"

"Yep. I want ice cream." She replies, pointing to the ice cream shop next door.

"Yeah, yeah. Let me get a coffee and then we will get you the ice cream I promised you."

"I was wondering where you ran off to." I say to him as I hug Juliet close to me.

He nods. "I went and took her off Mom's hands for a couple

of hours so she can pack and relax a little."

Bryan steps towards the counter and places his order, leaving Juliet in my capable care. She is, after all, one of my daycare kids and I spend just about as much time with her as I do with my own girls.

When he returns to my side, carrying my completed drink from the counter, Juliet reaches out to him.

"You're so good with her. She really loves you."

"Same for you. As soon as she saw you standing in here, she made a beeline right for you."

I look over my Juliet and gently tickle her tummy. "Well, this kid and I go way back." I say with a smile. "I'm glad she has you and that you're moving home. She will love having you nearby."

At the age of 18, Bryan joined the military. Since then, he's been gone from Fawn Creek, bouncing from one duty station to another. But, he has finally reached the end of that. In May, he will have completed twenty years of active duty and he will be retired. Over the summer, he purchased a piece of land with a mechanic shop on it. He plans to live and work on that land as soon as his current contract is up.

"I'm looking forward to it, too." He nods. "I've missed out on a lot with her and my mom and Avery already. May can't come soon enough."

I nod, just as the barista hands Bryan his drink. "Well, you two have a fun afternoon. I'm going to head up to my room and try to get some packing done. And maybe take a nap in the hammock on the balcony." I wave goodbye to Bryan and Juliet before leaving the cafe to head up to my room.

If Bryan is this good with his niece, I can only imagine how good he will be with his own kids. Too bad he and I can't be together, because that is enough to make him a catch in my book.

* * *

"Sorry we're late!" Avery's mom, Julie, says as she and Bryan make their way towards our table at dinner. Bryan, who is carrying Juliet, takes a seat across from me and smiles softly. Juliet is sleeping on his shoulder, with one hand wrapped around his neck and one gripping his beard.

I let out a soft chuckle. "You wore her out today."

"Yeah, I did," Bryan agrees, speaking softly to avoid waking her. "After ice cream, we played in the pool and the ocean. Plus, we built sandcastles. Then, we ate more ice cream, and she passed out in my room watching cartoons while I finished packing."

I let out a soft chuckle and shake my head. "That girl is going to be lost without you when we all go home tomorrow. Then, she will have to go back to reality with boring old Madi, who doesn't feed her ice cream three times a day."

"You are the furthest thing from boring." Avery interjects. "You guys are always doing such fun stuff at daycare. Between teaching them line dancing and playing in the mud and fin-gerpainting and baking. There's never a dull moment at your house. She is going to be miserable at home because she won't have Madi or Uncle Bryan. Just boring old Mom and Derek."

"Don't forget about boring old Grandma." Julie chimes in. "As soon as Bryan knocked on the door, Juliet forgot I existed and took off with him."

"You deserved a break, anyway." Avery chimes in. "Thank

you both for taking such good care of her while we've been here. I wasn't expecting to get much one-on-one time with Derek while we were here, but you guys made sure it happened, and that means a lot to us."

"It's the least we could do." Julie waves her off. "Thanks to you, we were able to come to Mexico and stay in this beautiful resort for free. I don't mind showing my gratitude with a little babysitting. Here and back at home."

Avery shakes her head. "I just still can't believe this is my life." She admits. "I never imagined that when I started making silly videos online that I would become an actual content creator. And I definitely never pictured getting a free wedding in exchange for content. Life is crazy."

"We are so proud of you for it, too." Tyler chimes in. "This has been so much fun, and it's all because of your hard work."

"And maybe a little luck." Avery adds with a shrug before turning towards me. "You ready to get back to reality?"

"Yes, and no," I say with a sigh. "I miss my girls. But, I don't want to go back to reality. Especially now that everyone in town already knows about my divorce. I wish I could go home and grab my kids and disappear for a month. Just until all of this blows over."

Avery reaches over and squeezes my hand. "You're going to get through it, friend. And we are all going to be there to support you. I promise it won't be long before everyone moves on from this and finds something new to gossip about."

"I hope you're right."

After dinner, our crew splits up, heading off in opposite directions, knowing most of us will call it an early night because of our flight home tomorrow morning. I'm making my way back towards my room, when I hear Bryan call out to me.

"Madi, wait up."

I pause and wait for him to catch up with me. "Hey, what's up?"

Bryan looks out towards the beach behind the resort. "You wanna go walk on the beach one last time with me?" He asks as he fidgets, running his fingers through his hair.

I look out at the water and then back at him. "I don't know. After last night, it's probably not a great idea."

"What? Are you afraid you won't be able to resist me? Afraid you might trip and fall into bed with me?" He teases. "Honestly, none of that sounds too bad to me." He reaches out to gently touch my hand, just as I spy Sierra and Cody come around the corner of the resort. I snap my hand back quickly.

I offer Sierra and Cody a wave and then watch them disappear down the hall.

"I better get going." I say, turning towards my room.

"So, that's it, huh? After spending all our free time together here, you're just going to avoid me now?"

I lower my voice. "I told you. Avery can't know about us. I can't take a chance of something else happening and her finding out."

"And you think avoiding me won't throw up red flags?" Bryan shakes his head. "Madison, I promise you. You are making this a bigger deal than it is. I like you and I know you like me too. No one is going to care if we are together."

I shake my head. "Bryan. We can't. It just won't work. Besides, you don't want to be my rebound after my divorce, anyway. I have a lot to work through before I can be in a new relationship, but even when I am ready it can't be with you. I gotta go. I'll see you in the morning."

Chapter 4

"Mommy!" Kenzi, my 4-year-old, runs screaming into my arms in my ex's entryway.

I squeeze her tightly and breathe in the scent of her lavender scented bubble bath. No matter how much fun I had on my trip, and how much I enjoyed it, I missed my girls so much it hurt. I smile down at my brown eyed, brunette daughter, gently smoothing her hair. These girls keep me grounded and keep me sane. I don't know what I'd do without them. I definitely wouldn't have survived the divorce.

"I missed you so much, baby girl. Did you have fun with Daddy?" I ask, slowly pulling back from our hug to look into her eyes.

Kenzi's head bobs up and down enthusiastically. "Yes. But, I missed you. Why did you go on vacation without us? Kate and I want to go to the beach too. I want to build a sand castle. And play in the waves like we did that one time."

"Because." Hisses Kate, my six-year-old, as she joins Kenzi in the entryway. "Mommy needed a break from us, so she left us with Daddy." She says, crossing her arms in front of her chest. "Right, mom?"

I scowl, taken aback by what my daughter just said. "No, Kate, that's not true at all." I assure her, stooping down to get to eye level with her. "I did not need a break from you. In fact, I missed you so much. Remember, I told you girls I was going to a wedding?"

"Well, that's what Daddy said." Kate shrugs, turning back to look at her father, who has since joined us in the entryway, for confirmation before continuing on. "He said sometimes Mommy's and Daddy's need a vacation from their kids."

I glare at my ex-husband, and take a deep breath, "Well, your father was mistaken. I would have loved to take you with me, but it wasn't possible. We will take a vacation someday, though. I promise."

Unfortunately, even as the words are leaving my mouth, I have a feeling that I am a liar. Sure, I can say that I'm taking the kids on a vacation, but how will that ever be a possibility? I'm a single mom now. It's enough of a struggle for me to pay my bills, but the chances of a vacation? Even if I can figure out how to pay for it, I don't know that I could drive to the beach alone with two kids, or navigate an airport with them. It's going to be a while before I can make good on my promise, but I will. One way or another.

This is just one more way that Ben totally and completely screwed me over. His selfish ways and the inability for him to keep his penis in his pants really ruined a lot of things for us. But one thing he will not be doing is turning my kids against me. Not over my dead body.

I stand to face Ben, literally and figuratively biting my tongue. There's no use in arguing with him over what he told the kids. He will either tell me they misunderstood him, say that they made it up or he will try to convince me that is exactly what I said as I was on my way out the door. This isn't my first rodeo with him. It's no use. The only reasonable choice for me is to repair the damage with Kate and Kenzi when we get back home... and start saving for some sort of vacation for them. Suddenly, the stuffed sea turtles and sand from the resort gift shop I brought home to them doesn't feel like nearly enough.

"Go get your things, and then we will head home." I tell the girls before turning my attention back to my ex. "Thanks for keeping them." I say to Ben.

"Did you have fun?" he asks, but he doesn't wait for my response before continuing. "Hey, do you remember that time we were in Mexico and took that catamaran and went snorkeling? You had too many margaritas, and you wore that tiny hot pink bikini..."

I hold up a hand to stop him from continuing on. "Ben, I have no interest in reminiscing about the good old days with you. Especially when those memories are from our honeymoon."

Ben huffs and shakes his head. "This hasn't been easy on me either, Madison. This whole town is against me. Last week, I tried to go to The Burger Shack to order dinner. I pulled up to the drive-thru window and Brenda wouldn't serve me."

I raise a brow and fight the smirk on my face. "What do you mean, she wouldn't serve you?"

"She pointed at the 'We reserve the right to refuse service to anyone' sign and then turned and just walked away. She completely ignored me and left me sitting in the drive thru."

I bite my lip to fight back the laugh that I so badly want to let free.

"It's not funny." He rolls his eyes. "At first, I thought she was joking. I just sat there in the drive thru for two minutes until I finally realized she wasn't coming back. I can't even get a burger in this town anymore."

I lean in towards my ex-husband and whisper, ensuring our

daughters don't hear me. "Well, it serves you right. And sounds like you should have thought through what you were doing. It's a small town and people love to take sides, especially over something like this."

"I made a mistake." He argues.

I shake my head. "No, you made a relationship. And a baby. You ruined our family and you broke my heart."

"That doesn't mean you need to sick the entire town on me."

"Ben, I didn't. I didn't say a word to anyone except my close friends because I would rather not be the topic of town gossip. But you know how word travels around Fawn Creek. Maybe if you don't want people to say shitty things about you, you shouldn't be a shitty person."

Ben shakes his head in response, and I continue on.

"Besides, for being so worried about what people think you were in an awfully big hurry to tell the entire world about your new girlfriend. Maybe you should be in just as much of a hurry to tell the girls that they have a new baby brother."

Ben frowns. "Amber is the one that changed her status. I couldn't just not accept it. And I'll tell the girls. Eventually. I'm just not ready yet."

I roll my eyes. "Well, you need to get it done. I don't like lying to my kids about the fact that they have a new sibling, especially knowing that word will be getting around town even faster now that you've claimed Amber on Facebook. If you thought the town hated you before, just wait. I would have preferred for everyone to have stayed blissfully ignorant for as long as possible."

Just then, Kate and Kenzi make their way down the hall, pulling their small rolling suitcases behind them.

"You girls ready to go?" I ask, taking a step back from their

23

father and our heated conversation, while putting on a happy face. I take the girls' suitcases so they can walk to my van without dragging them down the gravel driveway.

"Need help getting out to the car?" He offers.

"Nope, I've got it." I snap back, a little more aggressively than I intend to, as I follow the girls out the front door.

After the short drive home, I pull into my driveway and climb into the backseat to unbuckle the girls from their car seats. Kate doesn't need my help anymore, but Kenzi still does.

"Mommy, did you really need a break from us?" Kenzi asks softly. Her big brown eyes staring deep into my soul as I lean in front of her, unbuckling her straps.

I finish freeing her from the five-point harness and pull her into my arms, holding her close to my chest. "Of course not." I assure her, patting her hair gently. "I love you both so much and I hate being away from you, even if just for a little while. Just not every trip is a kid trip."

"Then why did Daddy say that?"

"I don't know, baby."

I don't know why your father does most of what he does.

* * *

"Goodnight, ladies." I say, turning off the overhead light in their bedroom. "I love you."

"Love you, too." They reply in unison, snuggled into their beds with their new stuffed turtles from my trip.

I close their door and pad down the hall toward my bedroom. Upon entering my space, I'm greeted by my suitcase next to the bed and a sigh of relief that I took the rest of the week off of work. Now, I can spend the rest of the week, and this weekend playing catch up and getting ready to start our routine backup on Monday.

When Avery asked me to go on this trip, I knew I would have to work extra hard to budget for my time off. This is the downside to running your own business. If I'm not open, then I'm not making money. Money that I so desperately need to make in order to support myself and my children, now that all of that falls on my shoulders.

When I opened my daycare three years ago, it really wasn't my intention to bring in a huge income. It was mostly just something to do to keep myself busy.

When Kate was little, she was going to a great home daycare, and I worked full time at a call center in Owen, the next town over. Customer service wasn't my dream job by any means, but it was a stable income that paid for child care and helped pay our bills.

However, when we unexpectedly got pregnant with Kenzi, we were thrown for a loop. Our childcare lady retired, which was long overdue, but it didn't leave us with many other options for childcare. Especially in a town like Fawn Creek that has a population of 1,200 people. The likelihood of finding a spot for two kids was nearly impossible. Not that my paycheck from my full-time job would cover the cost of daycare for two kids, anyway.

So, we decided I would stay at home with the girls and get licensed to watch just a couple of kids. I figured if I could make enough money to cover our grocery bill and for us to have fun with the kids on the weekend, then it would be plenty.

And it was, at first, anyway. I took on just a couple of kids that Kate was friends with at her old daycare. Over time, I added a few more. Some I took on because of the childcare shortage in Fawn Creek and others because of my inability to tell people no. However, I was able to keep my promise to myself to keep my enrollment numbers low so I wouldn't be overwhelmed.

Of course, that all changed the day I got a message on Facebook from a woman named Amber confessing that she and my husband were not only having an affair, but were also having a baby boy. Suddenly, the proverbial rug was ripped out from under my feet. I could no longer just do this job for fun. Instead, I had to take this thing I did for fun money and turn it into an actual source of income so that I could support myself and my girls once I filed for divorce from my husband.

Luckily, my bills themselves are manageable. My rent is pretty low, because we are still in the starter house Ben and I purchased at nineteen. We snagged a fixer-upper for less than the cost of our monthly rent, using a big down payment my parents helped with. Even more luckily for me, Ben didn't even try to fight over the house. He knew what he had done was wrong, so he simply signed the papers agreeing to visitation with the girls on Wednesday evenings and every other weekend. Then, he packed his things and moved back in with his parents until he could find a place of his own.

Now he is living in the country like he always wanted. He was always so hellbent on a big house with lots of land, even if it was out of the budget. All he cared about was keeping up appearances. He was adamant that everyone thought we were doing much better than we actually were.

He tried to convince me several times to sell our little starter house and buy something bigger. I never could bring myself to leave the house where we brought our girls home from the hospital. I'm more than thankful for my stubbornness now. Otherwise, I would have been the one moving in with my parents until I could afford a place of my own. And my daycare? It would have been done for.

I take my suitcase from the floor and plop it on the bed, then unzip it to start the not-so-fun job of unpacking. Heaving the laundry bag over my shoulder, I trudge to the laundry room. I chuck my clothes into the washer, start the machine, and head back to my room to find a notification on my phone.

It's a message from Bryan.

All of us had exchanged numbers in a group chat during the vacation planning process. However, this is the first time he's ever messaged me directly. My stomach flips at the sight of his name, and I can't fight the smile that spreads across my face.

We're just friends. I remind myself.

Bryan: Hey. I just wanted to make sure you made it home okay.

Madison: Hey. Yes, I did. Just working on unpacking before I get ready for bed.

Bryan: Oh, so you're one of those people.

I furrow my brow before responding.

Madison: One of what people?

Bryan: You know, the ones that unpack immediately after getting home from vacation. I bet you already started your laundry, too.

I pause and turn in the direction of the laundry room. The sound of the tub filling with water rings through the house, proving his point.

Madison: There's nothing wrong with that. I like to get my life back in order as soon as I can. When do you unpack?

Bryan: When I get to it, I guess. Generally, I just get stuff out of my bag as I need it. I'll probably finish next weekend when I do the laundry. I don't mind living out of a backpack as needed. It's not like I took much with me, anyway.

Madison: You're giving me hives.

Bryan: I knew I'd get under your skin in no time.

Madison: Oh my goodness. I'm going to bed. Thanks for making sure I made it home safe. You're a good friend.

Bryan: That's me. King of the friend zone. Goodnight, Madison. Talk to you later.

Madison: Night.

I plug my phone into my freshly unpacked charger and lay it on the bedside table. Then, I fall onto my bed with a huff. Bryan's a good guy. If only that's all that mattered.

Chapter 5

I slow my minivan to a stop at the curb in front of my parents' house. It's Sunday evening, and we are here for our bi-weekly Sunday family dinner. I'm twenty-six and the oldest of three kids. My brother, Randy, is twenty-two and lives in Missouri. Nathan, the baby, is a Junior in high school. While Randy is rarely in town for dinners, I bring my girls over every other weekend, when they aren't with Ben, and the rest of us sit down for a meal together as a family.

I climb out of my van and help Kenzi out of her car seat. As soon as her feet hit the ground, she and Kate take off running into my parents' house. I attempt to follow them, but I'm stopped by my Mildred, the neighborhood busybody.

"Madison, hello!" The white-haired woman calls out to me, as she shuffles her way towards my car.

"Hi, Mildred. How are you?" I reply, making my way towards her to save her some steps.

Mildred may be pushing eighty, but I must admit she seems to get around pretty good for her age. She's wearing a long floral skirt and a white sweater. Her white hair looks freshly permed. It's apparent she's visited Sierra's beauty salon lately.

"I'm good, dear." She says, as we meet in the middle of the street. "I heard all about that no-good husband of yours.

I'm sorry to hear about that." She says, lowering her voice, as though the rest of the town doesn't already know.

"Oh." I say, feeling my face blush. "It's okay. I'm going to be just fine without him. Don't you worry about me."

"Well, that's actually what I wanted to talk to you about. Now, my grandson is single. He's a cute boy, and he has a job where he makes good money." She carries on as she pulls her phone from her pocket and swipes through the screens. "Just look at him." She holds the phone up to my face. "Isn't he a looker?"

I look at a photo of her grandson, who can't possibly be over the age of twenty-one, if that. I examine the photo of the guy wearing a light blue polo and khaki pants. He's a cute kid, but definitely just a kid.

"His name is Jake. I could give him your phone number if you'd like me to." She suggests.

I shake my head violently. "Oh, no. I don't think that's...."

"He's a good boy and there are really not many good ones around this town, you know." She interrupts me. "You should snatch him up while you can."

"No, I understand, and I'm sure he's great. I just... I'm not quite ready to date yet. I think I'm going to stay single for a while."

Mildred lets out a heavy sigh and shoves her phone into her cardigan pocket. "Fine, suit yourself. But when you change your mind, you let me know, okay? If he's still available, I'll put in a good word for you."

"You'll be the first to know. But really, I better get going to family dinner. I'll see you later." I promise, turning on my heel and making my way towards my parents' house. My dad is standing in the driveway, peering into the open hood of my brother's car when our eyes meet.

"Oh, the world traveler has returned!" My father calls out to me with a grin. He lowers his voice as I get closer. "What was that about?"

I let out a heavy sigh. "Oh, Mildred was trying to set me up with her grandson."

He chuckles and shakes his head. "Isn't he like 15?"

"I honestly wouldn't be surprised at this point." I say with a laugh before turning my attention to Nathan's car. "What's wrong with it this time?"

He shakes his head and uses an old shop rag to wipe his hands. "It's a twenty-year-old car."

"Well, that's what kids are supposed to have for their first cars, right?"

He closes the hood and leans against it. "You know, yeah, that's what I thought when you were the first one to drive. Now, ten years and three kids later, I'm tired of working on cars. Good thing he's the youngest, because the next one would probably end up with a newer vehicle than you have."

I scoff. "Rude. The youngest kids always get the best of everything." I tease. "Well, I hope you know we appreciate you tearing up your knuckles on our junk cars."

"I'm glad someone does." He says with a chuckle before looking at me. "What the hell are you wearing?"

I look down at my shirt and laugh. My dad and brothers are huge football fans. In fact, they are borderline obsessed with the Kansas City Chiefs. I, on the other hand, don't care about football. In fact, the only sport I ever cared about was cheerleading, which I did throughout Junior High and High School.

I chose cheer because I loved to make people happy. The

football and basketball games happening while I performed didn't matter to me.

This drove my dad nuts. He would ask for specifics on games, usually the away games that he couldn't come to. When I had no idea if we won or lost, his head looked like it might explode. All I cared about was doing our sideline dances without messing up.

Since high school, I have made it a point to collect the most random football team merch and I wear it specifically during football season for family dinner.

Tonight, I'm wearing a Green Bay Packers shirt with a giant wedge of cheese on it.

"What? Do you have a problem with my shirt? This is my new favorite team."

"The Packers?" He grumbles, shaking his head. "Why?"

"Because they wear cheese hats and I love cheese. Obviously."

My dad lets out a disgusted sigh. "Let's go eat. We need to get you inside before the neighbors see what you're wearing." He teases, motioning towards the house. "I think your mom made fajitas."

"With cheese?" I ask, fluttering my eyelashes.

"Where did I go wrong?" He groans.

Dad and I make our way into the kitchen. "Hey, Mom! It smells amazing in here." I call out to her.

"You made it!" she exclaims, obviously glad to see me. "I was wondering if you dumped the girls off and drove away. They came barreling through the house and right out the backdoor to play."

I shake my head. "No, I got cornered by Mildred. She was trying to set me up with her grandson since the whole town

32

knows the status of my love life now."

"Gross. Stop talking about your love life. Some of us don't want to lose our appetite." My brother Nathan says as he enters the kitchen. He makes his way to the pantry and pulls out a bag of chips. He's already shoved a few into his mouth before he turns around to look at us. "What?" He asks our mom, whose jaw is hanging wide open.

She frowns. "I'm literally cooking dinner." She motions towards the stove.

He shrugs. "I know. It smells great and made me hungry, so I came to get myself an appetizer."

"Eating chips in front of the open pantry isn't an appetizer." I retort. "It's a snack."

"To-may-toe, Toe-ma-toe."

* * *

After dinner, I help mom clean up the kitchen before we move to the living room to join the rest of the family. As I make my way towards the sofa, my eyes wander, examining the photos taken of my siblings and me over the years. Between the three of us, my mom has quite the photo collection happening here. It seems like every time I come home; I notice another one I haven't seen in ages.

I pause in front of the mantle to further examine them when one in particular catches my eye. It's senior night, and I'm on the football field in my cheer uniform with my parents. I lift the frame from the shelf and inspect it further.

"I always loved that picture." My mom says softly.

I nod. "Me too. It's crazy to think this was eight years ago.

So much has changed since then. I barely recognize myself." I mutter, feeling tears build into my eyes.

"Oh, you don't look much different at all since high school." My mom says, waving me off. "You don't even look twenty-one, much less twenty-six."

I shake my head. "It's not really about what I look like. It's more about what I feel like. This girl had no cares in the world. The only thing that mattered was learning my cheer dances and picking out the right outfit to wear to that weekend's field party." I turn to face my mom, who is staring at me. "I mean, I did also have to figure out a solid alibi, so I could tell you I was staying at a friend's house during the field party, too."

Mom shakes her head. "I can't believe I was that naïve."

"Me neither, honestly. But it made for a lot of great high school stories." I say with a laugh. "Sometimes, I just wish I still felt like her. I used to love dressing up cute and hanging out with my girlfriends. My hair was always curled, and I always wore a bow that matched my outfit. 85% of my wardrobe was pink. Now, I feel lucky if I remember to brush my hair before putting it back up in a messy bun. And the only pink in our house is what Kenzi wears or a few of my ratty old T-shirts. How did I get so boring?"

My mom moves towards me and pulls me into a hug. "Madi, you are far from boring. There's nothing wrong with getting older and building a beautiful life. Which you have done."

I nod. "I know. I just... I miss the me I used to be. It feels like my whole life revolves around being a mom."

"Oh babe, that girl is still in there. I know you'll find her."

* * *

"Good morning and welcome home!" Ava calls out across the house as she comes through my front door on Monday morning with her daughter, Piper.

Piper was one of my very first daycare kids. We met her when she went to daycare with Kate, and the two quickly became best friends. When our provider announced she was retiring, Ava was in a pinch, searching for someone to keep Piper. And that's where I swooped in.

Over the years, Piper and Kate have grown up together and have become very close. Piper is just as much of a fixture in this house as my two girls and I spend just about as much time with her, too. I wouldn't have it any other way.

Piper is the best kind of kid. Not only is she well behaved, but she's super smart and she has just the right amount of sass. Sure, sometimes she speaks her mind a little too freely, but she's only six and we are still learning about keeping some thoughts inside our heads. At least most of the time, what she has to say is funny.

Besides that, she's the kind of kid that marches to the beat of her own drum. She doesn't care if all the other girls are obsessed with dolls and playing dress up. She likes monster trucks and Spiderman and making mud pies. Her individuality is refreshing and truthfully, I wouldn't complain if I had a house full of kids just like her. I'm so lucky to have been allowed to watch her grow up.

"Morning." I call back from the kitchen where I'm standing at the stove, preparing breakfast for the kids. "Piper, do you want some pancakes before school?" I ask the blonde-haired girl wearing a Minecraft T-shirt.

"Yes please! With Nutella and sprinkles." Piper replies, before taking a seat on the couch to get lost in cartoons with the other kids.

"Piper. This is not a custom made pancake bar." Ava groans. "You get what you get and you don't throw a fit." She reminds her daughter, who has already tuned her out. "Sorry, being the only child probably makes her a little bit spoiled." She apologizes to me, obviously embarrassed. "We probably ruined her over Christmas break."

I wave her off. "It's fine." I assure Ava. "Piper knows I keep Nutella on hand for her pancakes. She and I share a common dislike for pancake syrup, and I'm the one that got her stuck on Nutella in the first place." I say, as I prepare Piper's plate. "Besides, I'd rather give her something that I know she will eat instead of worrying about her starving at school until lunch."

Ava smiles warmly. "Madison, thank you for taking care of her in the mornings and getting her off to school for me. I know it's probably a pain to add one more kid to the mix in the morning, but knowing that she can start her morning off by sitting down for breakfast makes my life so much easier. If it were up to me, she'd be eating a granola bar in the car every day on the way to drop off while we pull up at the very last minute. This makes our lives so much easier."

"It's no biggie. Besides, I think it's been good for Kate to have someone to do her morning routine with. It calms her nerves to have someone else to ride the bus with. Especially someone as confident as Piper."

I spread a thin layer of Nutella on a pancake and add a small amount of rainbow sprinkles before adding a scoop of mixed berries to a divided portion of her plate. I place Piper's plate down on the table and I'm just about to call to the kids that their food is ready, when I notice Ava eyeing me suspiciously.

"What?" I ask nervously. "Do I have toothpaste on my face

or something?" I ask, wiping my mouth.

Ava says, "You look different since you left."

"Oh. Well, I got some color while I was in Mexico. They mean it when they say the sun is different there." I say with a shrug. "Juliet, Piper, Kate, Kenzi... breakfast!" I call out to the kids, causing a stampede of tiny people's footsteps to come into the room. I help Juliet get situated into her booster seat before making my way back towards the kitchen sink to clean up from breakfast.

"No, that's not it." Ava shakes her head before leaning in and lowering her voice so the kids can't hear her. "You got laid, didn't you?"

Immediately, I feel the color drain from my face.

"What? No. Why would you say that?" I stutter, shaking my head quickly.

How can she tell?

"Bullshit." She laughs. "Who was it? Some hot guy on a bachelor trip? A stranger?" Ava wiggles her brows. "You had a one-night stand in Mexico with a random guy, didn't you? I didn't know you had it in you, Madi! But, good job! I'm proud."

"I don't know what you're talking about." I say, turning on the kitchen faucet and placing a bowl under the running water, attempting to avoid eye contact with my friend.

Ava lets out a loud gasp and gently smacks my arm. "It was Avery's brother, wasn't it? Oh, my gosh. How was it? Older guys can be fun. They usually have a trick or two up their sleeve."

"No." I sputter, probably a bit too quickly. "Nothing happened with Bryan. Why would you even think that? You are delusional, my friend." I tell her, looking over at the kids to ensure they are still eating happily and not listening in on our conversation.

Ava places her hands on my shoulders and turns me so that I'm facing her. "Because he was the only single guy in the group. You are in denial. That's fine. I'll be here when you're ready to come clean with all the dirty details. I'll be looking forward to it, actually. It'll be the most action I've even heard about in a while."

"Ava, there's nothing to come clean about." I assure her, rolling my eyes. "Sounds to me you need to find yourself a man, though. You are the one that needs to get some. It's apparently weighing awfully heavy on your mind."

She laughs. "Listen, I've been single so long that I've given up hope at this point. I'll just live vicariously through you while I focus on building my real estate business and raise my kid. Piper is a full-time job on her own."

I turn back towards my sink full of dishes. "I'm sorry to disappoint you, friend, but there's nothing going on in my life for you to live through. This is the first time I've been single since I was fourteen. For twelve years, Ben was all I knew, and my life revolved around him. I think it's time to do a little soul searching before looking for another relationship."

Ava nods. "Okay, but you just let me know when you're ready to come clean about what you did. I'll be all ears."

Chapter 6

"Good morning!" I call across Drip, Fawn Creek's downtown coffee shop, as I enter through the door and make my way towards the counter.

It's Saturday, and it's been just over a week since I got home from Mexico. The girls are with Ben and I ventured out of the house to get a coffee and maybe pop into some local shops.

Cassidy, the owner, who also is Sierra's mom, beams as she watches me enter the room. "Hey, beautiful! It's so good to see you!" She replies. Cassidy has a way of making everyone feel special. I expected as much when she first opened. That was right after pouring her blood, sweat, and tears into renovating the old diner into a fresh new place. But somehow, even a couple of years after opening, she has managed to not lose her excitement for the job. Cassidy is warm, welcoming and so personable. She was born to run this business; Fawn Creek is really lucky to have her.

"It's good to see you, too!" I reply, as I reach the counter.

"You look like you got some sun in Mexico! I'm jealous. I am already tired of freezing straight to my bones and it's barely even winter here."

"Coming back to this weather was so hard." I admit. "I'd give just about anything to be back on the beach with a mojito.

But, I guess a large, hot vanilla dirty chai latte will have to do for now." I shrug, handing over my debit card.

"You got it!" Cassidy says. Quickly, she rings up my drink and gets to work on firing up the espresso machine. "So, it was a good trip?"

"The best!" I confirm. "It was definitely hard to come back here to reality."

Cassidy nods and moves towards the counter before lowering her voice. "Hey, just so you know, speaking of reality, word is getting around about your divorce. I've already heard a few whispers around the shop this week."

I frown. "Of course. Well, I don't know if Sierra told you, but Ben is officially dating the woman he had the affair with. He even put it on his Facebook page. I was hoping this whole thing would fly under the radar, but he might as well have rented out the marquee sign at the Pizza Hut so he could announce our failed marriage to every person who travels down Highway 75."

"I'm sorry, honey." She says, as she finishes making my drink. She slides it across the counter and squeezes my hand tightly during the exchange. "You deserve better than that. Better than him."

I nod. "I know. And honestly, I knew about the woman for a while before I confronted him, so I had time to come to terms with it. I think the hardest part is facing this town, knowing they are whispering behind my back."

Cassidy shakes her head. "I have not heard a single person say anything negative about you. Every whisper has been in favor of you and against Ben. This town loves you and has your back." Cassidy lets out a low chuckle. "Ben might be better off moving away, though. This is going to be a hard one for people to forgive."

"If I wasn't sharing two kids with him, I'd agree."

She nods. "That makes it more complicated for sure. Hopefully, it'll all blow over soon."

"Thank you. I hope you're right." I reply, taking a sip of my drink. "Life is just so weird right now. I feel like being Ben's wife was part of my identity and now that part of me is just gone. I'm just not sure who I am anymore."

Cassidy leans across the counter and looks at me with sad eyes. "Oh honey, you are so much more than that. I've known you for your whole life. You have always been so sweet and fun. I remember watching you on the cheer squad. You always had the best facial expressions, and you were never too busy for all the little girls that looked up to you. Looking back, it's obvious now that you were made to work with kids."

I smile softly. "I'm loving my job right now. And I have so much fun with the kids. It hardly feels like work. But, then I look around my house and my clothes and my hair... I just feel so plain."

Cassidy shrugs. "So do something about it. Paint your walls, get some cute new clothes, change up your hair. The only thing stopping you is you. Make your surroundings a reflection of who you are and what makes you happy."

"Just like that, huh?"

"Okay, maybe don't go burn all your clothes and shave your head and repaint your entire house." She laughs. "Start small. Maybe redo your bedroom. You deserve a place that's just for you to enjoy. A room that is all yours."

I pause for a second to contemplate this. "You know what? That's a good idea. I think I'll run down to the hardware store and look at some paint colors. What could it hurt?"

* * *

I leave the coffee shop and continue my walk through down-town Fawn Creek until I reach Hansen's Hardware Store.

I fling open the door of the store, causing the overhead bell to chime loudly as I step inside. Immediately, I make a beeline to the back of the building to visit the paint department.

Unfortunately, this is a much more overwhelming task than I was prepared for. Who knew there were 756 different shades of the color white? Not to mention all the other colors.

"Need some help?" A deep voice cuts through my concentration, causing me to jump.

I turn towards the voice and find myself face to face with what has to be one of the most gorgeous men I've ever met, wearing a red employee vest. His employee name tag tells me his name is Trey.

"Yeah. No..." I stammer. "I'm just looking. Honestly, I don't know what I'm doing." I admit.

"Are you looking for any color in particular?" He asks, raising a brow.

"Not really. I just thought I'd see what jumped out at me."

"What are you painting?"

I shrug. "Actually, I don't know. Maybe my bedroom. Something. Just looking for a change, I guess."

The man crosses his arms in front of his chest. "So, let me get this straight. You don't know what room you're painting or what color you want."

"That about sums it up." I confirm, feeling my face blush slightly. "Listen, I did not know the paint department was going to be so overwhelming. I haven't painted in years. My husband... I mean, my ex-husband is the one that handled the paint buying last time. I told him to get white, he got white, and we painted the walls with whatever he brought home. I didn't realize there were so many options."

"And now you want, not white, but you aren't sure what." He laughs.

"Exactly."

Trey ponders for a moment. "Well, I have just the thing for you. Follow me." He says, motioning in his direction as he leads me towards the paint desk.

As I approach the desk, he crouches behind the counter and, when he resurfaces, hands me a heavy, black plastic rectangle.

"What's this?" I ask, examining the item.

"It's a paint fan deck." He explains, taking the item back from me. With a swipe of a finger, he unlocks the block and frees a collection of paint sample cards, all in order by color, and lays the fan in front of us. "Now you'll have almost every color that you can imagine. Take this home and ponder on what you like. Then, when you decide, just come back with the color name and number and we will mix it up for you."

"Oh..." I nod, looking at the rainbow spread out in front of me, before closing the fan deck and securing the latch. "Thank you. This is actually very helpful. I'll bring this back once I decide."

He waves me off. "Nah, keep it. We get a new one every year with new colors. That one is last years and was probably just going to end up in the trash anyway. We can only hoard so many of them back here." He says with a shrug.

"Are you sure I don't need to pay for it?"

"Positive." He replies with a wink. "But I wouldn't mind a trade."

I raise a brow. "What kind of trade do you have in mind?"

A smile spreads across his face. "How about the fan deck for your number? Maybe I could take you out to dinner sometime?"

"Um..." I ponder the question. "I'm going to be really honest. Dating isn't really on my radar right now. I just went through a divorce and, well, it's... complicated."

Trey shrugs. "That's fine. I didn't mean to pressure you into anything. Maybe we could just exchange numbers then? We can get to know each other and maybe when you're ready to date, you'll let me be the lucky one to take you out." He offers a soft smile. "Sorry, I hope I'm not being too forward. It's just that you mentioned your ex-husband and I think you're really pretty, so I figured I'd shoot my shot." He shrugs.

I consider his suggestion for a second. He seems sweet. What could be the harm in getting to know him? "Okay, what's the harm in exchanging numbers?"

Without a pause, Trey slides a paint card and pen across the counter to me. I pick up the pen and scribble my name and number down for him before sliding it back.

He reads what I wrote. "Madison. Nice to meet you. I'm Trey."

"I know."

He looks puzzled. "Wait, how do you know? Have we met before?"

I laugh and point at his chest. "Your name tag." I respond.

He glances down at the name on his chest and chuckles. "Real smooth of me."

"The smoothest." I agree. "Well, I better get going. I have a lot of paint colors to research. I guess I'll talk to you soon?"

"Yeah, you will."

"Okay. Thanks again for your help today."

"Anytime. Happy to help."

* * *

"Hey ladies! This place looks great!" Ava says, taking a seat across from me at a long folding table in the middle of Fawn Creek Floral. She looks around, admiring the fresh paint job and newly added boutique merchandise. "I knew the new owner would do a good job, but I honestly never pictured all of this."

Just recently, the previous owners of the forty-year-old floral shop in downtown Fawn Creek decided that it was time to retire and sell the family business. Luckily, it wasn't long before the new owner, Beth, a friend of Cassidy, put in an offer. She did a complete remodel and rebranding before opening just a few weeks ago. Tonight, she is hosting her first ladies' night.

Sierra looks up from her plate of snacks and nods. "Mom said that the new owner is really excited to turn this place into so much more than a flower shop. Hopefully, this event will go well, and if so, she wants to host monthly Ladies Craft Nights."

"That would be so fun." I say, perking up. "I love crafting and any chance to hang out with you guys. The idea of painting a highland cow freaks me out a bit, though. I am definitely not a painter."

"I'm sure it'll be great." Avery waves me off. "This is all about the time together, anyway. Besides, if we hate the final product, next month we can have a Ladies' Night Bonfire and destroy the evidence."

I can't help but giggle at the idea of us all standing around a firepit burning our cow portraits, when Beth stands in front of the class to get the party started.

"Okay ladies. Welcome and thank you for coming to tonight's paint and sip party. I'm Beth and I'm the owner of Fawn Creek Floral. We are going to get started here in about ten minutes. Don't worry if you aren't a great freehand painter. Tonight is being hosted by the talented Elaine, who will teach us step by step, how to create a masterpiece you can be proud of." She says, motioning towards a woman that's busy handing out paint brushes to each table. "Help yourself to a snack and don't forget to get something to sip on while you paint. We have wine, water, tea, soda and seltzers on the table over here." She says, pointing to the refreshment table. "Hopefully tonight will be a lot of fun and this will be just one of many Ladies' Night Events here at FCF."

"Well, how's everyone doing?" Ava asks, taking a bite of a massive chocolate covered strawberry. "What's new with everyone?"

Avery shrugs. "Not much here. Just working and content creating. And working on my mobile boutique. I had no idea stripping down an old camper would be so much work."

"It's going to be amazing when it's done, though." Tyler assures her. "That camper needed a new life and you are just the one to do it. What about you Madison?"

I shrug. "Today I started looking at paint colors for my house. I don't know what I'm doing, but I'm pumped to spruce up my place and ditch those dull white walls."

"Nice!" Ava says excitedly. "Where are you going to start?"

I shrug. "Maybe my bedroom. Cassidy actually suggested I start in there and create a space just for myself. I'm toying with painting the walls pink, but I don't know. What if I hate

46

it?"

"If you hate it, it's just paint and you can paint over it." Avery shrugs.

I turn to Ava. "What about resale value? Ben always told me we needed to just keep everything neutral, so it would be easier to sell if we ever wanted to."

Ava rolls her eyes. "Are you planning to sell in the next year?"

"No."

"Then, who cares? Like Avery said, it's just paint. You can always paint over it later. It's your house and you should create a space that you love. Don't worry about non-existent future buyers. Honestly, even then I tell most people not to waste money on paint. The new owners will probably want to repaint anyway, so it's not worth wasting your time."

"That actually makes me feel a lot better." I confess.

"Good. Stop living your life on Ben's terms. Do what makes you happy. Paint your whole house pink if you want. As long as it's what you want, that's what matters."

* * *

I step into my bedroom and lean my finished canvas against the wall before working on gathering my things to take a shower. Just as I'm about to leave the room, my phone pings to alert me of a text message. It's from our group chat.

Avery: Here's the group photo! Enjoy!

On the screen appears a photo of all of us girls with our finished paintings. They are... interesting, to say the least. No one will

47

ever mistake us for a group of artists, but we had a good time.

Bryan: I think you sent that to the wrong chat.

Avery: Damnit. Well, enjoy our masterpieces anyway. We are all available for commissions, for a fee, of course.

Ugh. This is the downside of having more than one group chat. We have one that we started when we began planning for Avery's wedding, and then one that is just for us girls. Avery has a bad habit of not paying attention to who she is messaging and sending things to the wrong chat way too often.

My phone pings again. This time it's a message from Bryan sent straight to me. I hate to admit it, but seeing his name on the screen causing a flutter in my stomach. Ugh. I hate to admit it, but I like hearing from him.

Bryan: You are quite the artist.

Madison: Are you laughing at me right now?

Bryan: No. Never. Scout's honor.

Madison: Were you even a Boy Scout?

Bryan: Of course I was. Do you think I'm some sort of fraud?

Madison: That is exactly something a fake Boy Scout would say.

I glance back down at my canvas. The example of the painting was a highland cow with a rose in his mouth. Mine looks more like an emo cow with the shoulders of a linebacker.

Madison: It's not that bad.

Bryan: It's kind of bad.

Madison: Sigh. I know. But it was fun!

Bryan: Then it was worth it. You should hang it up so you will remember the night you had.

Madison: Maybe I'll give it to you as a housewarming gift. Then you can always remember this talk.

Bryan: Oh, I couldn't take that fine art from you.

Madison: Oh, I think you could. It may be worth millions one day. And it's rude to refuse a gift.

Chapter 7

"Bye girls. I love you and I'll see you Wednesday." Ben calls to Kate and Kenzi as they make their way past me and down the hall to their room. It's Sunday night and the girls are finally back at my house after a weekend with their dad.

"Bye dad, love you!" They reply in unison, without so much as slowing down, leaving me standing in the doorway with their father. The last place I want to be.

"Well, I'll see you Wednesday." I say, standing in the doorway as I hold on to the door, ready to close it as soon as he clears the threshold.

However, Ben stops me by holding his hand out to stop the closing of the door. "Oh, hey, Madison. I noticed that the light above the garage door is burnt out."

I frown and stick my head out the door, eyeing the space above my garage door. Just as Ben had said, the area beneath it is pitch black. I sigh heavily. It's always something around here that needs to be taken care of.

"Well damn. Thanks for letting me know. I'll take care of it tomorrow."

"I'll take care of it now. I'm already here." He offers.

The thought of him spending my extra time in my house does not sit well with me. "I don't know if I have any bulbs. I'll probably have to go get some. So, thanks anyway."

"They're in the garage in the cabinet. I'll take care of it for you." He says, pushing past me and then making his way across the living room. He's already making his way through the kitchen before I realize what is even happening.

So much for this space being my own. Honestly, I'd rather pay a handyman to come change a bulb for me than allow Ben to do me any kind of favor. Instead, I turn on my heel and make my way to the girls' room to see them.

"Hi. How was your weekend?" I ask, leaning against the door frame as the two girls sit on the floor, already lost in their extensive Barbie collection.

"Good!" they reply in unison, without even lifting their eyes to look at me.

"Daddy took us to Sonic for ice cream before we came home." Kenzi offers.

I attempt to hide my scowl. Of course, he would bring them home all sugared up on a school night. However, I'm not going to say a word about it. They aren't acting crazy. I got some time alone and they are playing harmoniously, which is a rare occurrence around here.

Instead, I turn back down the hall and make my way towards the living room when I hear Ben re-enter the house through the garage.

"Done!" Ben calls out to me, entering the kitchen. "Anything else you need me to take care of for you while I'm here?"

I'm bracing myself to come face to face with him again when the sound of his heavy footsteps stops on the kitchen linoleum.

"Madi, are you painting something?" He asks.

"Yep."

"What? The girls' room?" He continues to pry, still shouting from the kitchen.

This piques interest in my two Barbie fans, even all the way across the house. Both girls run into the living room and stop in front of me.

"Can you paint our room?" Kenzi asks, excitedly squirming. "I want pink."

Kate scowls. "No, Kenzi. Pink is for babies. I want turquoise." She demands. "Mom, tell her I'm the oldest and I get to pick."

"Girls." I say, holding up my hand. "We will talk about this later."

"What if you paint two walls pink and two turquoise?" Ben suggests, resting against the doorway, as though he has any say about the color of this house. He crosses his arms in front of his chest and smiles.

"Yes!" Kenzi shouts, jumping up and down with excitement now.

"No! That's not fair!" Kate argues, sticking out her lip. "Mom, can I please have my own room?"

I furrow my brows and look at my oldest daughter. "Your own room? Really? You don't want to share a room anymore with your sister?"

"No, I don't." Kate deadpans, causing Kenzi to burst into tears before running to their room.

My eyes dart back to Ben, who is now staring at his phone while still leaning in the doorway. He looks up just in time to see me staring.

"Oh, sorry. What'd I miss?" He asks.

I frown. "Nothing. You better get going. We need to get bedtime routines done." I turn to Kate. "Tell your dad bye and go jump in the shower."

"Can we talk about my room?" She asks, raising a brow.

Giving me a sure glimpse of what her teenage years will look like.

"Yep, we will talk after your shower." I promise her, before offering a soft smile.

"Yay!" Kate squeals and runs to her father. "Bye!" She says, giving him a hug before running towards the bathroom.

As soon as I hear the water start, I turn to face him, crossing my arms in front of me. "Seriously, did you have to start all that?"

"All what?"

"The painting talk. Now Kate wants her own room and Kenzi's feelings are hurt." I let out a heavy sigh. "What should have been an easy evening of getting them ready for bed has turned into a bunch of drama that I have to deal with."

Ben throws his hands up. "My bad. I didn't know it was going to be such a big deal to ask you a question."

"Maybe if you would have just left like I asked, the kids would still be playing happily and my night wouldn't be a disaster."

"Sure, blame it all on me," Ben says, shaking his head. "Whatever makes you feel better. I just wanted to help you."

I narrow my eyes and plant my feet, glaring up at my ex-husband. "Well, I don't want your help. I want you to go home."

With that, Ben turns and makes his way towards the door, but then he pauses and turns back to me.

"Madi, I'm sorry I hurt you. I truly am, but eventually you are going to have to forgive me. You can't blame every little thing that goes wrong on me. Like it or not, we are going to have to co-parent together for another fifteen years. Are you planning to hold on to all that anger towards me until then?"

I shrug. "Maybe. We will just have to see how it goes, I

guess."

"Madi..."

"Please, just go. I have a lot to take care of around here."

"Fine." He breathes out heavily. "Kate, Kenzi... I'm leaving. Love you!" He calls down the hall.

"Love you, too! Bye!" Kenzi calls back, still obviously crying in her room.

Kate, who is in the shower, yells "Bye" over the sound of the running water.

With that, Ben walks out the door and into the dark winter night and, once again, I clean up his mess.

* * *

By ten o'clock, I have both girls calmed down and sleeping peacefully. I'm showered and cuddled under a blanket on my couch, with an episode of Gilmore Girls queued up on the TV.

This is my regular nightly routine, more often than not, since Ben left. While I don't miss him, I admit I miss the warmth of someone else next to me in bed. Trying to sleep alone in my bed has been a struggle, and I've found it's much easier not to fight it and sleep on the couch instead. Maybe once I get my room done, I'll find it easier to sleep in there. At least that's my hope.

When the girls got tucked in, I had them both content with bedroom plans. Kate's new room will be where the guest room is now, across the hall from the room the girls have shared all their lives. It doesn't get used much anyway other than as a storage space for daycare things. The girls have just always shared a room because I thought they liked to be together, but it's fair for Kate to need her own space now that she's getting older.

Kenzi is calm after being promised that she can redecorate her room to look however she wants. Now I have two bedrooms to repaint and redecorate on a budget. Meaning, my bedroom can be slid to the back burner for a bit.

Just as I get lay down and begin to pay attention to what's happening in Stars Hollow, my phone vibrates. I smile before picking it up. Part of me admits that I'm hoping it's Bryan. He and I have spoken just about every day since leaving Mexico, but it has been purely platonic. He has respected my boundaries and while it's hard; I know it's the right choice.

However, it's not Bryan. It's Trey.

Trey: Hey, how's it going picking paint colors? Sorry, I haven't had time to message you lately. It's been busy around here.

Madison: No worries. I'm a mom, remember? If anyone understands being busy, it's me. Paint color picking was great until it was disastrous. Now my daughters both want their rooms painted, too. This has turned into an expensive project.

Trey: It doesn't have to be. You can use my employee discount. Just let me know when you want to come by.

Madison: Really? Won't you get in trouble?

Trey: Lol. No, it's fine. It's one perk of being a partial owner in the store.

Madison: That's really nice of you. I could come by Wednesday after my daycare kids leave. The girls are with their dad that night.

Trey: Sounds great. Maybe I could take you out to dinner

afterwards?

 Madison: It's a date.

Maybe what I need to distract myself from Bryan is a date with someone else. It's worth a shot, isn't it?

Chapter 8

"Thank you again for doing this." I tell Trey, as he helps me place the cans of paint into the back of my van.

Thanks to his employee discount, I have an assortment of pink, turquoise, and sage green paint. Every room in our house will be soon undergoing a makeover. If we didn't have plans for a date night, I'd go straight home and get to work.

He reaches up to close the hatchback on the van before turning to face me with a smile. "Hey, I'm happy to help. What do you say I follow you home and we can drop off your van? Then you can ride with me to Owen to grab dinner. Unless you wanted to stay in town?"

"No, Owen's great." I say immediately, checking my watch. Honestly, I'm relieved to know that our first date will not be happening in the fishbowl that is Fawn Creek. I want to ease into this new life as quietly as I can. "I just need to be home by eight-thirty to be there for my girls when they get back."

"We better get going then." He says with a grin.

"I'll lead the way."

Within ten minutes, I'm sitting in the passenger seat of Trey's Ford Fusion and we are headed out of Fawn Creek, towards the nearby town of Owen, Oklahoma.

"Anything in particular you're in the mood for?" he asks.

I think for a moment. "How about hibachi? I haven't had that in a while."

Trey looks at me. "Wait. What? A woman that knows what she wants to eat? Are you an alien?" He teases.

I can't help but chuckle. "I guess so. Sorry, I haven't done this dating thing in a while. Was I supposed to pretend like I don't care where we go?"

"No, this is great. Refreshing even. It's nice to go on a date with someone that doesn't play mind games and make me guess what she's wanting."

I feel the heat rise in my cheeks. So far, my first date is going better than I imagined.

"Besides." He continues. "I've never had hibachi."

I scoff and make a show of clutching my hand over my chest. "Well, then that sounds like it's settled. You can't possibly go through life without experiencing hibachi. Get ready for the experience of a lifetime."

"How can I say no to that then? So, what's going on the rest of this week, besides painting?"

I shrug. "Well, I have a hair appointment. Besides that, nothing. Just working."

Trey raises a brow. "A hair appointment? I hope you aren't planning to cut that long, beautiful hair of yours."

I pick up the ends of my long, dirty blonde hair that are draped over my shoulder and examine them. "Actually, yeah. I was planning to cut it to my shoulders and add some high-lights."

"I just wish you wouldn't do that." He shakes his head disapprovingly. "I really like your hair. I mean, I'm not telling you what to do, but I think you're going to regret it."

I raise a brow at Trey's comment but decide to change the

subject instead of arguing about my hair. I (and my parents) learned a long time ago that I'm just stubborn enough to be offended when someone bosses me around, therefore causing me to do the exact opposite of what they are saying. It's too early in the evening, and our relationship to argue over my hairstyle.

Instead, I change the subject. "So, what do you do for fun?"

"I like cross fit. I go four days a week." He says, noticeably flexing his forearm that's draped over the steering wheel. "Besides that, I'm a diehard football fan."

"Oh, who do you root for?"

"Babe, I don't just root for the Chiefs. I bleed red and yellow." Trey says, almost in a bragging tone. "What about you? Who is your team?"

I shake my head. "To be honest, I don't have one. Football's not really my thing."

"Really?" Trey raises a brow.

"Yeah. I mean, I cheered in high school, but I really didn't even pay attention to it back then either. My dad and brothers are big Chiefs fans, too. We usually do family dinner on game nights. I really just go for the food, though."

"Huh." Trey mutters to himself.

"Regretting this date yet?" I tease, gently pushing his arm. I can definitely tell that he is into CrossFit when my hand pushes against his bicep. This must be what the women on the covers of romance novels are so excited about.

Trey chews on his bottom lip as though he's considering it, but turns to me with a smile. "No." He answers quickly before pulling into the parking lot of the hibachi restaurant. "You hungry?"

"Starving."

* * *

"Thank you." I say to the hostess as we take a seat at the large U-shaped table surrounding the open grill in the hibachi dining area, alongside a family of six.

"It's my sister's birthday. She's sixteen." Says the little girl I'm seated next to. She can't be older than six years old.

"Oh, happy birthday." I say to the teenage girl seated next to her.

"Thanks." The brunette teenager smiles awkwardly through her braces.

"Why are we sitting with some random family?" Trey whispers, leaning in to me.

"Oh, it's just the way it works out when you come in with just a couple of people. They need to squeeze enough people in to make it worthwhile. It's no biggie, and it can be a lot of fun."

"I guess if you think sitting next to other people's snotty kids is fun. Not really what I would have in mind for a first date, though." He admits.

Snotty kids. I can't explain it, but the way he says that really annoys me. Of course, that's probably just because I love kids and don't mind getting to know them. However, the girl beside me is far from snotty. She's sitting politely in her seat, chatting with her sister, the birthday girl.

"It's fine." I hiss back to him as the server comes to take our drink order. "This will be a lot of fun."

Before the waitress is even walking away from our table, Trey has his phone out. He's watching a reel with the volume up higher than necessary. I glance over at his screen just as he scrolls to the next video.

I take a deep breath and try to make the best of the situation. At least I got my first date out of the way, right? Surely it couldn't get worse than this.

Finally, the server reappears with soup for each person at the table. At least this will give me something to occupy myself with while my date is busy.

She places a bowl in front of Trey, and he leans down to glance into the bowl with a disgusted look on his face. As soon as she walks away, he turns to me. "What is this shit? And why is there one random mushroom floating in it?"

I chuckle. "It's onion soup. And it's really good." I say, using my miniature ladle spoon to take a sip. "Try it."

Trey follows suit, but grimaces as he brings the liquid to his lips. "So weird. Who would want to eat that?" He mutters, sliding the bowl away. "I hope the rest of this food is better."

And suddenly, I can't wait for this night to be over.

* * *

By the end of dinner, I can see why Trey is still single. Besides him rolling his eyes every time the family next to us spoke, complaining about how his steak was cooked, and just looking bored out of his mind during the dinner show, he also refused to leave a tip. Luckily, I had a twenty-dollar bill in my purse that I slipped to the server on my way out the door.

"Well, I can sure say I haven't been missing out on anything by not having hibachi." Trey laughs as he leads me towards his car.

Personally, I had a great meal, as always, but it's not worth arguing about. All I have to do is get in the car and make it home. Maybe having our first date in Fawn Creek wouldn't have been so bad after all. At least then I wouldn't have to spend thirty more minutes alone with this man child.

Trey and I make it to his car and he follows me around to the passenger side door. I step off to the side, assuming he is being a gentleman, and opening the door for me. I couldn't be more wrong.

"So." he says, reaching out to grab my hand and pulling me in close against his body. "The food may not have been great, but I think we are both hungry for something else, anyway." He mutters, just inches from my face as he uses his body to trap me between him and the car. "What time are your kids going to be home?"

I pause and look down at my watch. "Umm... soon. We probably better get going."

He nods and then looks down at me, using the back of his hands to gently stroke my face. "That's okay. I could always come back after they go to bed."

I swallow loudly. "I don't think that's a great idea."

Trey chuckles and leans down to kiss me. I move and narrowly crawl out from between him and the car. He turns to face me with his hands on his hips. "What's wrong with you? I thought we were having a good time." He scowls.

I pause. How do I explain to this guy that I have to ride home with that I would rather he not touch me? Ever. He doesn't wait for my response.

"Madison, don't you kind of owe me something? I mean, I bought you dinner, and I got you a discount on paint..." He trails off.

"I'm not a hooker, Trey." I say, slowly taking a step back

from him, towards the restaurant.

"I know that. I just thought that maybe it would be a fair trade."

"Um, no. It's not." I let out a heavy sigh.

Trey shakes his head and turns back towards his car. "Good luck finding a ride home then, bitch." He calls out before slamming the driver's side door shut. With that, he squeals his tires and speeds away.

* * *

"Oh my gosh, thank you for picking me up." I say, closing the door of Avery's SUV and buckling my seat belt. "What a nightmare."

"No problem. Now, can you please explain to me how you got stranded at the hibachi restaurant with no car?" She asks, as she puts her SUV in drive and makes her way out of the parking lot.

I let out a heavy sigh. "Basically, the date from hell."

Avery raises a brow while staring out over the steering wheel. "Wait, back up. I didn't even know you were dating."

"Well, this was the first and probably last date I'll ever go on. I think I'd rather just die alone if that's what I have to look forward to."

"Who did you go out with?"

"Trey Hansen?"

Avery deadpans. "From Hansen Hardware?"

"Yes..."

"Shit. Madison. New rule. No going on dates without clearing it with me first. Actually, just ask the group chat so

63

we can all approve. Our group has collectively been on enough terrible dates that we should be able to save you some stress."

I frown. "In my defense. He seemed perfectly harmless."

"Yeah, he's good at that," Avery agrees. "Trey is an over-grown man child. His dad has busted his ass for thirty years building that hardware store from the ground up and all Trey has done in return is take advantage of his dad's success and cause him problems. He's an entitled prick, and I won't be surprised if he runs his dad's business into the ground as soon as he takes over. I hope he wasn't too awful towards you."

I groan. "Well, he was great until the date actually hap-pened." I say, shaking my head. "I should have known he was a jerk when he told me I shouldn't cut my hair because he likes it long."

Avery scowls. "Ew. Why do random men think we care what they think of our hair?"

I throw my hands in the air. "Right?!" I exclaim. "Glad to know I'm not the only one annoyed by that. Anyway, it was all downhill from there. He was complaining for the entire meal about the family we sat next to. They were fine. The little girl next to me was so polite and he was acting like she was a heathen. He complained about the food. He was watching reels instead of getting to know me. And that was all before the first course was served."

"He must not know that you are like the preschool whisperer. Kids flock to you. They love you."

"Right? And I love it. I'm glad kids like me. It's job security." I say, rolling my eyes before going on. "Anyway, he was just obnoxious. Making faces at the onion soup and refusing to eat the vegetables. I mean, I understand not wanting to catch broccoli in your mouth when the chef throws it at you, but it's fun. I caught mine on the first try and he was so embarrassed. And don't get me started on the saki."

"In his defense, I don't like the saki being sprayed in my mouth either." Avery laughs.

"Sure, but acting like the rest of us at the table are cavemen is wild. He thinks way too highly of himself."

Avery shakes her head. "I still don't understand how you ended up stranded, though."

"Oh! That was the best part. Once we got out to his car, he tried to kiss me and invited himself over to my house after my kids go to bed tonight." I shake my head. "He told me I owed him for buying me dinner and getting me a discount on paint." I groan. "When I told him no, he called me a bitch and left me stranded. Not that I was going to get in the car with him, anyway. I'm so glad you were in town."

"Holy crap. I'm so glad you're okay." Avery pauses, searching for an appropriate response. "At least your first attempt at dating is past you and surely it can only get better from here. The next one will be less traumatic, I'm sure."

"At this point, I'm not sure I want a next one." I admit, sinking into the seat of the car. "Maybe I'm just meant to be alone after all."

Thanks to Avery, I made it back home just in time to meet Ben with the girls. I get the kids into the house and get their bedtime routine started before making my way to my bedroom. Even though Trey didn't really get much of an opportunity to touch me, I still feel dirty. I can't wait for a shower. As I toss my phone on my bed, it vibrates to alert me of a text. It's Bryan.

Bryan: Hey. You okay? I was just talking to Avery, and she said she had to rescue you from some dude tonight. Do I need

to come kick someone's ass? Because I will. I might be old, but I'll happily fight someone.

I read his text and can't decide if I should laugh or cry.

Madison: No need to break anyone's nose. I just went on the date from hell, and luckily, your sister was close to drive me home.
    Bryan: Are you sure you're okay?
    Madison: Yes. I'm okay. Seriously. I'm home safe and sound. Thank you though.

I pause for a second and stare at my phone before firing off one more text.

Madison: Hey Bryan. What would you think about me cutting my hair?
    Bryan: Why would I care if you cut your hair?
    Madison: I don't know, just curious if you had an opinion on it.
    Bryan: Madison, you could shave your head bald and I'd still think you're the sexiest woman I've ever met.

Chapter 9

Ding, dong.

At 8:45 on Thursday morning, the sound of the doorbell chimes through the house, causing a stir of excitement among my daycare kids.

I jump from my spot on the floor, where we are finishing up circle time to make my way towards the door.

"Carolyn! Good morning. Thanks so much for coming." I say, letting her inside the house. "I really appreciate you."

Today is my hair appointment with Sierra. Carolyn, my neighbor, is here to substitute for me while I'm gone.

She waves me off. "No problem at all! I have been looking forward to this ever since you asked me. I have plenty of things planned for the kids today." She says, pulling her canvas tote bag from her shoulder and giving me a peek inside. The bag is filled to the brim with books, homemade play dough, toys, and what appears to be a container of cookies.

"You are so good to them." I chuckle. "And they love having you here. They've been looking forward to seeing you all week."

I grab my coat and purse from the hooks hanging in my living room and turn back towards the kids.

"Okay, friends. Miss Carolyn will be here with you for a few hours today while I get my hair done. I expect all of you to be on your very best behavior while I'm gone. Got it?"

"Got it." The chorus of children confirms.

"We will be just fine." Carolyn interjects. "Go. Enjoy your day and don't rush back. I've got this under control." She adds, taking a seat on the rug in the living room and pulling out a collection of books to read to the kids.

I wave goodbye to the kids once more and then sneak out the door, into the cool winter air.

* * *

I park my van at the curb in front of TBR, Tyler's downtown bookstore, just before 9:00 and head inside.

A couple of years ago, Andrew bought this building. What was once a rundown piece of slab with fire and smoke damage from the building that burned down next door, is now an incredible piece of property.

The first floor of the building holds Tyler's bookstore. The second story, accessible by stairs or an elevator, houses Sierra's salon and Ava's Real Estate office. For a long time, this building seemed like it would sit empty forever, but Andrew and Tyler poured their hearts into turning this place into a beloved part of Fawn Creek.

I fling open the door and step inside to see Tyler sitting at the desk, holding a cranky baby Molly.

"Good morning." I say with a smile. "I have an appointment with Sierra upstairs, but I just thought I'd check and see if my new book has come in yet. It's the new Abby Jimenez one."

Tyler looks towards a pile of unopened cardboard boxes in

the corner behind the checkout counter. "Yes! I believe it is in one of those. They came in late yesterday and I haven't had a chance to unpack them yet. But I promise I'll have it ready when you get done upstairs. I know you've been anxiously awaiting that one." She says, as Molly fusses again.

"Thank you so much! I'm excited to start on it tonight. By the way, just so you know, I have space for Molly if you ever decide that you are ready for her to come to daycare."

Tyler picks up a half full baby bottle from the counter and gives it a shake. "Thanks, Madi. I really appreciate it. I just don't think I'm ready to take the plunge into daycare yet."

"I get it and no pressure. I just want you to know that the option is there if you need it. Even if you need to just drop her in for a few hours. I know being a mom is a lot of work. Balancing a baby and a successful business must be exhausting. I'm here if you need me." I check my watch. "But now I've got to get up to my appointment with Sierra. I'll see you soon."

I make my way up the wooden stairs and then enter through the antique frosted glass door that leads into Fringe. Sierra is standing behind her salon chair, working away on a familiar Fawn Creek resident.

"Hey, Sierra. Hi, Mildred." I greet the ladies as I take a seat on an old church pew in the waiting area.

"Hey!" Sierra smiles brightly. She's adorable today in her denim overalls and a long sleeve kelly green top that really sets off her curly red hair. "I'll be with you in just a second. We are just finishing up."

I wave her off. "No worries. I'm in no rush today." I say, pulling my current read from my purse and settling in to read a quick chapter.

"Thank you so much for making me feel beautiful." I hear

69

Mildred tell Sierra as she stands from the chair and digs in her brown leather purse. She pulls out a check and hands it to Sierra. "I'll see you in two weeks. Same time?"

"Yes, ma'am." Sierra confirms. "You're so welcome. Have a good day."

Mildred shuffles towards the door and then turns back to look at me. "Madison, have you thought any more about my grandson?"

I shake my head. "No, I'm sorry Mildred. I'm just still not quite ready to date yet."

"Suit yourself." She huffs and turns to leave the room.

We listen for her to climb onto the ancient elevator and begin her descent downstairs before discussing what just happened. I turn to Sierra and shake my head. "She is adamant that I'm going to date her grandson, Jake. It's not happening."

"Isn't he like seventeen?"

"Maybe? His photo sure makes him look like a baby. After my date from hell last night, I'm probably never dating again, anyway." I confess.

"Pause." Sierra says, holding up a hand. "Let's decide what we're doing to your hair and then you better be ready to spill all the details."

"Buckle up, friend. It was a crazy night."

Over the course of the next forty-five minutes, Sierra meticulously paints my hair with a soft brush and wraps the color in foil, while I give her the full rundown of the previous evening's events.

"Well, I can see why you never want to date again." Sierra shakes her head. "What a jerk. But please don't let that stop you from trying again. Madi, I promise there are good guys out there. You just might have to do a little searching."

I frown, looking at the reflection of my foil covered hair. "Sierra, I don't know. I'm starting to think that the dating pool is full of pee. Honestly, if a guy my age is still single, it's for a good reason. He is a cheater, or an alcoholic or a narcissistic jerk or..."

Sierra nods. "Yes, it's true that there are a lot of losers out there, but you will find a good one. I'm sure of it. You deserve a happily ever after and I know you are going to get one."

Sierra takes a seat across from me and pulls out her phone. "Want a coffee? I'm going to text my mom an order and I'll go grab it while you process. You've got another half hour to go."

"Yes. Caramel Macchiato please. I'll give you some cash." I say, getting up to grab my purse and handing her a ten-dollar bill. "Anyway, that's enough about my awful love life. Tell me how you and Cody are doing."

Sierra smiles brightly. "We are great. Never better. Our house is coming along great and we are really enjoying building it together."

. Cody and Andrew, his brother and Tyler's husband, went in together a couple of years ago to buy some land outside of Fawn Creek. Andrew and Tyler built a barndominium on their piece of land. Cody and Sierra built a shop nearby, and they have been living in that while they work on building their dream house next door. The rest of the land is being used to raise cattle.

"I bet it's great to live next door to family," I gush dreamily, "And just think, when you have babies, your kids can grow up together."

Sierra's expression immediately changes and her body tenses. It's almost as though someone flipped a switch. "I'm going to go grab our coffee. I'll be back." She says, throwing

71

her purse over her shoulder and disappearing out the door before I can speak again. I listen as the sound of her feet thud down the old wooden staircase, carrying her way from our conversation.

What did I say wrong?

* * *

While waiting for Sierra to return, I pull out my phone and snap a quick selfie with my foil covered hair. I post it on my Snapchat and before I can even put my phone away; I have a response from Bryan. Our group used the app to communicate while we were in Mexico and I forgot I even had him on there.

Bryan: You're beautiful. Even in a tinfoil hat.

I blush and fire off a message telling him thank you, just as Sierra comes back in the door with a coffee in each hand. She hands me one and I take a sip while she checks under a piece of foil to see how my color is processing.

"Just a few more minutes and we will wash you up."

"Great. I can't wait to see it."

"And you sure you want shoulder length hair? Once I cut it, I can't bring it back."

I pause for a second to ponder her question, remembering my conversation with Trey. Just the thought of him telling me what to do with my hair, makes me want to cut it even more. "Yes, and not just because I want to do it despite Trey." I say with a laugh. "I'm ready for a big girl haircut."

"It's going to look so good." Sierra takes a sip of her coffee and then looks back at me from her seat in the nearby wash chair. "Hey, Madi. I'm sorry I froze up and ran out the door earlier. That was rude of me."

I wave her off. "It's okay. I'm sorry if I hit a nerve. I really didn't mean to."

She shakes her head and blinks quickly to fight back tears. "It's not your fault. Baby talk just gets to me. Cody and I don't want kids." She confesses. "That was the first thing we agreed on when we started dating. We just want to be married and enjoy life together. But everyone seems to think we are delusional for not wanting to start a family. It sucks, because I know my mom would be such a great grandma. But, I just don't want to. Am I a terrible person for not being maternal?"

I shake my head. "No, of course not. If you don't want to have a baby, that's okay. And your mom will be okay. She has plenty of other random kids in Fawn Creek to spoil. Do what's right for you. Besides, you are the perfect person to be a really fun aunt."

Sierra moves towards me and gives me a hug. "Thank you, friend. That's exactly what I needed to hear. Now let's get you finished up."

Chapter 10

"Thanks so much for the makeover and the therapy session." I call out to Sierra as I walk towards the door to exit the salon.

Sierra looks up from the hair that she's sweeping up from the salon floor.

"Anytime, friend! It was as great of a therapy session for me as it was for you. Have a good day!"

Carefully, I make my way down the wooden staircase and enter the bookstore once again. This time I'm greeted by a smiling baby Molly and a much more refreshed version of Tyler.

"Madison!" she squeals upon seeing me. "Your hair! I love it. Sierra is a magician, isn't she? That makes me want to do something new and exciting with mine."

"She really is. Thank you. It's going to take some getting used to, but I love it." I say, absentmindedly finger combing the fresh curls Sierra gave my shortened locks. "Is my book ready for pickup?" I ask, glancing towards the now empty box next to the counter.

"Yes!" Tyler says, leading me towards the counter and handing me a paper bag with her logo stamped on the front. "I've heard that this one is so good."

"I bet it is. RomComs have been my thing lately. I can't get enough."

"Well, I don't blame you." Tyler smiles softly. "Life is tough. RomComs make it better."

I nod. "They really do. Why face reality when instead you can stick your nose in a book and forget that reality even exists?"

"Exactly." She agrees with a laugh. "We could all use a little more of that."

I pay Tyler and thank her before I make my way out of her shop. Then, I step onto the sidewalk before pulling out my phone to text Carolyn and check in.

Madison: All done!How's it going there?

Carolyn: Great. They are sleeping and I'm reading a book. Take your time, honey. Grab yourself some lunch. I hear the grocery store has Chinese food today in their deli. It's so good.

Madison: That does sound really good. Want me to bring you some?

Carolyn: Oh no, I ate before I came and I have a roast in the crockpot for when I get home. Thanks though. Seriously, take your time. I'll be just fine here.

Madison: Okay, see you soon.

I slip my phone into my coat pocket and walk down the street towards the grocery store, Fawn Creek Market. It may be the middle of January and the coldest time of year in Kansas, but today it almost feels like a spring day. In fact, my coat is almost too much for this weather.

I finish my walk and step into the market. There I'm greeted by Avery's mom, Julie, as she strolls by with her shopping cart.

"Madison! I love your hair." She gushes. "Did you just get it done?"

I smile and instinctively reach up to touch my freshly cut locks. "Oh thanks! Yes! Sierra just finished it for me. I'm just grabbing lunch, then heading home. I got a substitute for the day." I say, as though I need to explain why I'm out during the daytime instead of at home with her granddaughter.

"Oh, that's great. I'm glad you could get away and get some self care time. You deserve it." She says with a smile, pulling me into a hug before I even realize what's happening. "Sorry, I'm a hugger." She explains, still holding on to me.

"Never apologize for being a hugger." I say. "So am I. You can randomly hug me in the grocery store any time." I add with a soft smile.

"Be careful. I'll take you up on that." She laughs. "Okay, I'll let you go. It was good seeing you."

"Good seeing you, too. Bye!" I say, as I make my way towards the deli at the back of the store. I approach the counter and place my order before stepping out of the way to wait for it to be prepared. I pull my phone from my pocket and see that I have a notification from Bryan, in response to the selfie I posted of my new hair.

Bryan: Looking good.
Madison: So you approve?
Bryan: I already told you. I'd approve, no matter what your hair looks like. But, yes. I really like it. It's sexy as hell. I never could have imagined you could get hotter than you already were.

I feel my face redden as I read the text from Bryan. I've been called a lot of things over the years, but I can't remember ever being called sexy. Not even by my ex-husband. I pause, trying

76

to decide how to respond when I'm interrupted by a deep voice calling out to me across the store.

"Madison King, is that you?"

I turn towards the sound of the voice and spot the familiar face of Kevin Howard, a guy I've known since we were in preschool together, but haven't seen since high school. "Kevin, hi. How are you?" I ask, as he makes his way towards me. He's wearing a blue flannel shirt and tight wrangler blue jeans on top of his scuffed cowboy boots. I have to admit. He looks great. Just as great as he did when we were teenagers. Not that I would have ever had the nerve to talk to him back then. I also can't help but notice the absence of a ring on his finger.

"I'm good. Long time no see." He says with a smile that could easily bring a girl to her knees. "How are you doing?"

I shrug. "I'm great. Just grabbing some lunch before heading back to work. Are you still living over by Pawhuska?"

"Sure am. I have a small ranch over there that keeps me busy. I just ran into town today to help my parents with some things on their land. What about you? What have you been up to?"

"Not much at all. Just staying busy. Raising my girls and running my home daycare."

His eyes glisten as he leans in towards me. "Hey, I'm sorry to hear about you and Ben, by the way. For what it's worth, I think he's a dumbass for messing up a good thing with you."

I let out a heavy sigh. Ben is the last thing I really want to talk about right now, or really any time, for that matter. But, I suppose this is the newest gossip in Fawn Creek. Until some other scandal happens, I am going to remain the star of the show. "Thanks Kevin. It is what it is, I suppose. I'll be just fine."

"I know you will." He says, offering me a smile as he reaches behind him to pull his wallet from his back pocket. He hands me a business card. "No rush, but when you're ready to move on, let me know. I'd love to take you out sometime and get to know you better."

My eyes widen as I take the card from his hand. This is the last thing I was expecting when I saw him today. Teenage me would die right now if she could see the hottest guy in school giving me his number. "Oh, um... thank you." I reply, stumbling over my words.

Kevin blushes slightly. "You know, I always had a thing for you when we were in high school. Truthfully, I've had a bit of a thing for you since Jr. High, but ole Benny beat me to the punch. I figured I'd get a chance eventually, but then the two of you ended up together for a lot longer than I think anyone actually expected. I'd hate to miss my window again."

I pause before swallowing loudly and stuffing the card into my back pocket. "Well, thanks." I say awkwardly. What are you supposed to say when someone tells you they had a crush on you before either of you could drive? Just then, a voice calls out over the store loudspeaker.

"Madison King, please make your way up to the customer service desk. Madison King."

Kevin and I both turn to look at the speaker overhead, as though it'll provide some kind of information about why I'm being paged.

"Well." I say, blushing. "I guess I better get going." I say, picking up my lunch from the counter. "Um... it was nice seeing you."

"You, too. Take care. Don't forget to call me." Kevin says before turning and making his way towards the cooler at the back of the store.

I can't help but to watch him walk away, with his tight jeans accentuating his backside on his way out. As soon as he's gone, I shake my head, still reeling from the experience, as I make my way towards the front. When I get there, I find Julie and Tyler's mom, Lisa, standing at the customer service desk, whispering quietly to one another.

"Hey. Do you know why I was paged?" I ask, inching closer to them.

"It was me," Lisa answers with a shrug, as though this is something she does daily.

I narrow my brows. "Wait. Do you work here?"

"No." she says, grabbing my arm and pulling me in close before she whispers the next part. "I saw you talking to Kevin, and I just had to intervene."

"Intervene?" I ask, my eyes darting between the two ladies just as Kevin makes his way to the checkout counter to buy not one, but two cases of beer.

We pause and wait for him to finish checking out before we awkwardly wave goodbye. Finally, Lisa continues. "Honey, I know he's a good-looking boy, but you need to steer far away from him."

I frown. "Really?"

Julie nods, as though to say she agrees. "He's nothing but trouble."

I furrow my brows. "Trouble? How so?"

Lisa shakes her head and leans in close to me. "Well, you didn't hear it from me, but he's got a bit of a problem with the bottle, if you catch my drift. His mother is in my Sunday School class, so I hear all about his problems first hand. He's been arrested for public intoxication and driving under the influence, not to mention the jail time he's done for domestic violence." She frowns. "It really is a shame because he's a beautiful man with a great family, but alcohol has a strong grip on him. And when he's drinking, he is not someone that his mama is proud of."

I grimace before leaning to the side to remove the business card from my pocket and quietly dropping it into a nearby trash can. The last thing I need is to get involved with anyone that has drinking problems.

"Good choice." Julie says, as she watches the card fall in the wastebasket.

"Thank you both for the heads up. The last thing I need is to bring an alcoholic into my life. Especially with two little girls around."

"Besides." Says Julie, gently nudging me with her elbow. "I think there is another man out there much better suited for you anyway."

"I better get going." I quickly change the subject motioning to the checkout counter. "You ladies have a good day."

* * *

Madison: Guess who I just ran into?

Bryan: Michael Jackson

Madison: Your mom.

Bryan: Hopefully not with your car. Otherwise, my sister is going to be pissed.

Madison: I saw her at the grocery store. She was trying to convince me not to go on a date with a handsome cowboy and go out with you instead.

Bryan: She's a smart woman. You should listen to her.

Madison: If only it were that easy.

Bryan: Listen Freckles, the only one that's causing this to be difficult is you. All you have to do is give me the word and I'll come running to sweep you off your feet.

Madison: Maybe in another life, Bryan. I don't see how that's possible. Honestly, I think friendship is the best for us. Dating is probably not a good idea for me right now.

Bryan: Okay, then I'm not going to beg you. I'll give you space and I'll stop chasing after you. But, when you're ready, I hope I'm the first one to cross your mind.

Chapter 11

Two weeks later

"Yay Myrtles!" Kenzi squeals excitedly as I put my van in park in front of our favorite store in Fawn Creek, Myrtle's Market.

Myrtles is not your typical flea market, instead it's so much more. Inside the walls of the two thousand square foot store, you can find everything you need, as well as so much that you didn't realize you wanted. With over fifty vendors showcasing everything from boutique finds to hand made soaps and everything in between, it's impossible to walk out empty-handed. Not to mention the fact that it's owned and operated by one of the best mother/daughter duos in Fawn Creek.

Over the last two weeks, I have worked away during nights and weekends to repaint all three of our bedrooms. After selling off our old decor by posting it on Facebook, the girls and I are at Myrtles today to find some new decorations for our new rooms.

"Hi girls!" Starla, the owner, calls out as my kids and I make our way through the entryway of the store. "Out doing some shopping today?"

"We are looking for decorations for our rooms!" Kenzi tells her, smiling proudly. "Kate and I have our own rooms now, so I want to hang pictures of unicorns on my walls. Do you have any unicorn pictures?"

I shake my head. "Hey Kenzi, Starla can't possibly know everything that's in this store. It changes all the time. Let's just go look and see what we can find."

Starla, however, is drumming her hands on the bright turquoise countertop where the cash register stands, obviously searching her memory. "Actually, I think in the back room we have some unicorn decorations." She tells Kenzi with a wink. "But you never know, there may be more than that."

"Thank you!" Kenzi squeals, her face lighting up. "Let's go, Mom. We have lots of unicorn hunting to do."

Thirty minutes later, the girls and I have finished making our rounds through the store. We make our way to the checkout counter with arms and a shopping basket full of goodies.

"Looks like you found a few things." Starla chuckles as the girls and I work to pile our finds on the counter.

"Just a few." I say with a laugh. "I can not believe how much stuff the girls found for their rooms."

I finish piling our finds on the counter, just as something catches my eye and begs for me to check it out. I make a beeline to the north wall of the room and inspect a hot pink romper that's hanging on the wall. It's cute, and it's my size.

"Mommy, that's so beautiful!" Kenzi squeals. "Are you going to buy it? It'll make you look like a princess!"

"I... I don't know. I think I'm too old to wear this."

"Too old?" Krystal shakes her head. "No, it's cute and it'll look great on you."

"Really?" I furrow my brows. "I don't know."

"Do it." She nods. "You're never too old to wear what makes you happy."

I stare at the outfit again and contemplate it. It's a far cry from the scrubs I wear every day for work and the legging and T-shirt combo I wear the rest of the time, but I admit. I love it.

I've always been curious about trying on a romper, but the one time I mentioned it, Ben quickly dismissed the idea. He told me I was too old to wear something like that.

"Go try it on." Starla suggests. "The girls will be just fine here with us."

I look to Kenzi and Kate for confirmation. After they offer nods of approval, I carry the hanger and quickly make my way towards the bathroom.

As soon as I close the zipper, I stand back to look at my reflection. I fall in love. It's not too short, or too revealing. It's soft and comfortable and the bright pink fabric immediately lifts my mood. Quickly, I take it back off, redress and carry it to the checkout counter to add to my pile.

"Okay, fine. I'll take this, too." I say, carrying the hanger towards the cash register and handing it to Starla before I can change my mind. "I'm sure I'd regret leaving without it."

Starla and her daughter, Krystal, work quickly to ring up our items.

"So Kate, I take it you found a few things too?" Starla asks, holding up a sign with a video game controller on it.

"Yes! I found some Taylor Swift signs and some gamer pictures." She says, proudly. "My room is going to be so awesome. Like a teenager's room."

I groan. "Let's not be in too big of a hurry to be a teenager, okay? You have plenty of time left to be a little girl."

"Fine." she grumbles as I hand Krystal my debit card to pay for our purchases. "My room is still going to be awesome, though."

"Yeah it is." I agree, tucking away my card. I hand each girl some things to carry and load up my arms with the rest of our finds. "Are you girls ready for some lunch?"

Kenzi groans dramatically. "Yes! Shopping makes me hungry."

* * *

"So, are you girls excited to go home and hang up your new decorations?" I ask, reaching for a chip to dip in my bowl of salsa at Rio Escondido, Fawn Creek's Mexican restaurant.

Both of the girl's nod happily, with mouths full of chips and salsa.

"Mommy, do you need to call Daddy to come over and hang our stuff up for us?" Kenzi asks thoughtfully.

I furrow my brows. "No, of course not. I know how to do it."

"Are you sure? Daddy used to be the one that did that stuff," Kate adds. "Do you even own a screwdriver?"

I pause, considering the question. "Actually. It's called a screw gun, and no, I don't have one of my own. But that's okay. We can borrow grandpa's." I say, pulling out my phone to fire off a text to my dad.

"But you know how to use it, right?" Kate asks, raising a brow.

Before I can answer, Ava and Piper approach our table.

"Hey guys!" Ava says with a smile, as Piper runs over to hug Kate. "What are you ladies up to today?"

"We just got done shopping for our rooms." Kate grins excitedly to Piper. "It's going to be awesome."

"And now mommy is going to borrow my Grandpa's gun when we get done eating." Kenzi adds.

85

Ava's eyes widen as she turns to face me. "A gun? You okay?"

I shake my head, nearly choking on the chip I just put in my mouth. "A screw gun." I say, a little louder than intended. "We are going to get a screw gun so we can hang up our new decorations." I add, shooting Kenzi a look. I can feel the rest of the restaurant staring at us. "What are you girls up to today?" I ask, trying to ignore my suddenly gained attention.

"I had two showings this morning and one this afternoon." Ava shakes her head. "It's been a busy day."

I turn to Piper. "Have you been assisting your mom all day?" I ask.

Piper nods.

"She's been a great helper." Ava smiles. "It probably helps that I found my old Game Boy in my mom's attic and it still works. She's been playing Super Mario all day."

"I'm going to beat it before the weekend is over." Piper adds smugly.

"Well, we aren't doing anything else today. If you want to bring her over before you go to your afternoon showing, feel free." I tell Ava. "I'm sure the girls would love to have her."

"Mom, please?" Piper whines. "I want to show Kate my game."

Ava looks at me and then back at the girls. "That's fine with me. As long as Madi really is sure she wants an extra kid in her house today. If I babysat every day, I don't know that I'd want extra kids on my day off."

I wave her off. "If it gives my girls someone to play with, it's more of a win for me than anything." I laugh. "Besides, it's Piper. She's a great kid and never a problem at all." I add, just as our food arrives. "We love having her around."

"Okay, that settles it. We will see you this afternoon."

* * *

"Okay ladies. We are just here for some screws and nails. Then we will stop at Grandma and Grandpa's before we go home." I say. "Do not ask for anything else. We blew our budget this weekend already on all the stuff we got at Myrtles."

"Okay." They both reply in unison.

We make our way into the store and I stop short when I see Trey working at the cash register. "Damnit." I mutter under my breath. Sure, I knew there was a chance of running into him here. It's a small town and surely there aren't that many employees here, so the odds were stacked against me. However, I had hoped that it would be his day off. Unfortunately, in our small town, there is nowhere else for me to go to get what we need, so I have to just face my fears.

I guide the girls towards the hardware before turning back to look at him. He doesn't see me. Instead, he seems to be very distracted talking to a leggy brunette. Quickly, I work to gather what I need, grabbing some screws and a box of drywall nails that my dad had recommended via text to me while we were eating lunch.

Then, we make our way up front to face Trey.

"Oh, hi," He says, greeting me with a tone that almost sounds like he is annoyed to see me.

As if he should be the annoyed one.

"Hello." I say, trying to keep a steady voice while putting the things down on the counter.

"My mom is borrowing a gun," Kenzi announces. "Because she can do things herself and she doesn't need my daddy's help."

"Oh." Trey's eyes widen and he finishes scanning our items.

"She's just talking about a screw gun." I mutter.

"Got it." He nods before looking up at me. "So, I see you cut your hair,"

"Yep." I confirm, pulling my card from my wallet.

The silence at the counter is deafening as I wait for the card to process. As soon as it's done, I take my receipt and grab my bag. I lead the girls out the front door without saying another word to Trey.

"How do you know him?" Kate asks, scrunching her nose.

"We used to be friends." I say, sparing my six-year-old the gory details of my dating life. Or lack thereof.

"Why aren't you two friends anymore?" Kenzi asks.

"We just aren't." I say, shaking my head. "Some people are just not good to be friends with."

"I'm glad you're not friends with him anymore." Kate tells me, as I help her get into the van.

"Why?" I ask.

She shrugs. "I don't know. He just doesn't seem very nice."

I guess when they say that kids and animals can read people; they aren't wrong. I climb into my van and buckle my seat belt, pausing as the memory of the day I met Bryan pops into my head.

I let myself think back to the day of the Christmas festival. Back then, Ben and I were still married, but even then, I knew something was off. He was never present for family activities anymore. He took every opportunity to go to work that he could. Little did I know he was with her the whole time. Not working overtime like he told me he was. My life was falling apart, and I was clueless and more lonely than I'd ever felt.

The day of the Christmas festival, I was a mess. Ben and I

were fighting a lot. I didn't want to take the girls into public by myself, but I would not make them miss out on seeing Santa because of my issues.

We were running late, and we got to the festival to line up to see Santa just in time to be in the back of the line. As if it couldn't get any worse, Kenzi was twirling in line, as she often does, and she fell onto the street scraping her knee. If Ben had been there, one of us could have taken her to the car to clean up the boo-boo, while the other waited in line with Kate. That's the way it would have been handled in any previous year, but of course, that year was different. It was all up to me. Kate didn't want to get out of line and miss seeing Santa, and I couldn't blame her. We were already late and now this. Just as I was trying to figure out what to do, Bryan and Avery swooped in. Bryan picked up Kenzi, found the local pharmacist that was off duty, and got him to open his store to use his first aid kit. Within minutes, Kenzi was back with her tears all dried up, holding a sucker for herself and one for her sister. For months Kenzi wanted to know where my friend was that helped her at the Christmas festival. She could immediately tell that he was good. And for good reason.

Bryan had saved the day. I was a stranger to him. He knew I was friends with his sister, but not that I was Juliet's babysitter ever since she was born. He had no idea how rough things were for me. And he didn't have to. Bryan simply did the right thing. He saw what was wrong and jumped right in to fix it.

I think about that day all the time. That little bit of kindness in the darkness is exactly what I needed, and he showed it to me while expecting nothing in return.

When I saw him in Mexico, that's all I could think of. And I admit, it made me want to get to know him better. Everyone

89

else, except his mom, of course, was there with their significant other. By default, we ended up spending a lot of time together. I got to know him, and the more I knew, the more I found to like about him.

That's when I knew he was different. That's when I knew I wanted to get to know him. Now, a month after we've gotten home and back to normal, I can't help but wonder. Would it be so bad to give us a chance? Maybe he's exactly what I need. But what would Avery think?

Chapter 12

I wave to the girls as they are making their way into Ben's house, while he holds the screen door open for them. After they disappear, he looks up at me and offers me a small wave. Despite the urge to roll my eyes, I wave back and roll up my window before backing out of the driveway and pulling away.

Nothing about the last few months has been easy. Even though I knew the divorce was coming long before I filed the papers, I still admit that the finality of it all stings. Ben and I made a promise to each other. We agreed to be together through thick and thin. We agreed to put our marriage first. Those vows? They meant the world to me. However, they apparently weren't nearly as important to him.

I never wanted to raise my kids in a divorced household. I never imagined that the boy I fell in love with when I was a teenager would do this kind of thing to me. We were supposed to grow old together. We were supposed to raise our kids and then spoil our grand babies together. Ben chose instead to step outside of that agreement. He had an affair. He created a child with another woman. Now all the promises and plans that the two of us had made have vanished. Every plan, every dream that I had for my future involved him. And now here I am, alone, trying to figure out what my new future looks like.

Now instead of the family time that we used to have every weekend, here I am, dropping off our girls at his house and going home to spend the weekend alone.

Instead of our usual pizza and movie night, I'm settling for take out from the Mexican Restaurant and junk food from the gas station. It's six o'clock on a Friday night and it's obvious that most of the town had the same idea to stop at the Gas & Go before heading home.

I make my way into the crowded store, and quickly get to work at finding my weekend snacks. It isn't long before I have my arms filled with a bottle of Diet Dr. Pepper, Sour Patch Kids, and a large bag of caramel cold brew M&M's. Satisfied that I have all I need, I make my way towards the counter. I join the line behind several others and wait patiently for my turn.

Until I hear a familiar voice whisper into my ear. "Hey there, gorgeous."

The heat of his breath on my neck sends a shock through my body. I don't have to turn around to know who is standing behind me. *Bryan.*

It's been just over two months since we last spoke. Since the day I told him that we could never be together. Two months since he told me that he would stop chasing me. And he did, just like he said.

I let out a heavy breath and try to calm my racing heart before turning to face him. Why did his voice cause my stomach to fill with butterflies? Why do I want to throw my armload of junk food on the ground and climb him in the middle of a gas station? Lord, help me.

My eyes meet his and his mouth forms into a crooked grin. He knows what I'm thinking about and I wish he didn't.

"You alright?" He asks.

"Yeah. I... I just didn't expect to see you. I didn't know you were coming to town."

He shrugs. "I would have told you, but you wanted space. So, I gave you space."

I nod. "Right."

"My house got delivered this week." He explains. "I had to come down this weekend to sign off on it. And I had some furniture delivered today. So, I loaded my truck up with boxes from my place in Texas and here I am."

My eyes widen. "Your house! Have you seen it yet?"

"Yeah, just left there and then came into town for some pizza and beer." He says, showing me the pizza box in his hand.

"Dinner of champions."

He nudges his head towards my armload of food. "Look who's talking."

I narrow my eyes and glare at him. "Do you have a problem with my dinner? Are you saying I should be on a diet?" I ask in a teasing tone, before turning away from him and moving up in the line.

Bryan chuckles before he leans forward and whispers over my shoulder. The feel of his breath on my neck nearly causes me to melt into a puddle, right in the middle of the gas station. "Madison, I love every inch of your body. The only thing I'd change about it would be to take it out of this store and back to my place."

His words cause my breath to hitch and I feel my skin grow warm. I can only imagine my face is glowing bright red and I'm thankful that I can't see the overhead store mirror in order to confirm it. How did I let him get to me like this? Why do I want it to keep going? I have no problem telling myself that

93

nothing can happen between us until I'm face to face with him. Suddenly I hear this voice, and every bit of my common sense is out the window.

I let out a barely audible groan as it becomes my turn in line. I step up to the counter and put my things down. While the cashier is ringing up my items, I keep my back to him. Trying to hide the fact that he has got me completely flustered. I complete my transaction and then step aside for him to do the same.

"Well, I better get going. It was nice seeing you." I say.

"I'll be home all weekend." He informs me. "Maybe you should come check out the new place."

I swallow hard at the thought of being alone with him. "That's probably not a good idea." I confess. "See ya," I add, before making a beeline from the store and climbing inside my van. Once the door is closed, I push the ignition button, only for my vehicle to do nothing other than make a clicking sound. "You have got to be kidding me." I groan as I try the ignition once more.

Nothing.

I pick up my phone and scroll for my dad's contact listing. Just as I'm about to click on his name, a knock on my driver's side window causes me to jump. I turn to find Bryan peering in at me. I sigh and open my door. "Yes?"

"Having trouble?" He asks. The flirty expression on his face has been replaced with a look of concern instead.

"I'm fine. It's just not starting. I'm going to call my dad and see if he can come help me."

Bryan frowns. "Pop the hood. I'll look."

I shake my head and pick up my phone, scrolling to my dad's name. "You don't have to do that. I'm sure you have better things to do."

"I'm not going to leave you sitting here alone. Let me at least look."

"I'm not your problem." I argue. "Your pizza is going to get cold."

"I have a microwave. Stop being so damn difficult, Madison. I'm a mechanic. I know what I'm doing. Just pop the freaking hood."

"Fine." I grumble, reaching forward to pop my hood.

Bryan disappears around the front of my van and reappears after a couple of minutes.

"Your battery is dead. I'm going to jump you real quick."

I pause, looking back at him, trying so hard to ignore the sexual innuendo.

He lets out a sigh. "I'm going to jump start your van with my truck, you perv. Sit tight." He replies with an eye roll. It's not long before he has moved his pickup next to my van. He gets out and pops his hood before stringing the jumper cables between our vehicles. "Okay, go ahead and try it!" He calls out to me.

I once again try to start the van, and this time it works. Bryan closes my hood and swings back around to my window.

"Thank you for your help." I say.

"No problem." He offers, leaning down into my vehicle. "Are you headed home?"

"I'm going to go pick up my dinner first and then I am. Why?"

"Don't turn the van off when you go get food. Leave it running or it might not start again. And just text me if you need me. I'll be around all weekend."

"Um.. okay. I'm sure I'll be fine."

"If it happens again, I want to know so I can look at it. You might need a new battery or there may be a problem with your alternator."

I let out a heavy sigh. That's the last thing I need to hear today. There is one mechanic in town. Jonathan Sanderson. Jonathan just so happens to be best buddies with my ex-husband. Once upon a time, I thought he was a good guy. However, he proved himself wrong when the truth about my ex-husband came out and not only did he take Ben's side, but he let it slip that he knew about the affair all along. Ever since then, I just don't feel like I can trust the guy. I mean, how do I believe that he's a man of integrity when he willingly stood by and watched what Ben was doing? I'm going to have to find a new mechanic. And I was hoping it wouldn't have to be so soon.

Which means that I will probably have to travel out of town for that. Long gone are the days when the town mechanic could come to my house and pick up my van to change my oil while my daycare kids are napping. Even if I felt like I could stand to see the man face to face, I couldn't give him my hard-earned money without wanting to vomit. I've lost all respect for him.

Of course, I could ask my dad. Even though he's already told me he's tired of working on our cars. Surely, he would still do it.

"Hey, you still in there?" Bryan interrupts. He's still leaning against my window.

"Yeah, I'm just trying to think of how I'll get that fixed, if the alternator is the problem."

"Me." Bryan offers. "This is what I do for a living, remember? I'm going to open my own shop when I move home, and it won't hurt me to start now. I can change your alternator with no problem. Don't stress about it."

"Don't you need tools?" I ask, raising a brow.

"Madison, I don't need much to change an alternator and I already have 75% of my personal stuff here. I'll take care of it."

I frown. "But you're here to worry about your own stuff. Not to work on my car."

Bryan lets out another heavy sigh. "Madison, will you stop being so damn stubborn? I want to help you. Let me."

I nod. "Okay. Thank you. Hopefully that won't be necessary, but I appreciate it."

"Okay, remember, don't shut the van off until you get home. Try it tomorrow morning and let me know how it goes."

"Okay, thanks again for your help." I say with a nod before placing my van in reverse and backing out of my parking spot. "See ya later."

Please God, let my van start tomorrow. I do not need to spend any more time with Bryan that I have to. I don't know if I can control what happens if I do.

* * *

The chiming of my cell phone rattles through my living room and wakes me up from a deep sleep. I sit up on my sectional sofa and search for the lost electronic, praying that there's nothing wrong with the girls. I remember the days when I could go without being tied to my phone 24/7. Before, when I'd hear a text notification on a Saturday morning, I could easily ignore it. Those days are long gone, at least while the kids are gone. Now every chirp from my phone fills me with fear that it's something from Ben. My mind always races to the chances of a broken arm or a high fever or maybe just a little girl that misses her mommy. I don't want to miss an opportunity to be there for my kids if they need me.

Finally, I locate the device and hold it in front of my face. I let out a relieved breath when I see that it's a message from Bryan.

Bryan: Hey, when you get around to it, make sure your van starts please.

Madison: I'm sure it's fine.

Bryan: I hope you're right. However, I still need you to check please.

Madison: I'm really not your problem.

Bryan: I never said you were. However, there is going to be a cold front next week and I'll be damned if I let you be stranded somewhere with two kids because your car won't start. Just please do this for me. Without arguing. Or I'm coming over.

Madison: You don't know where I live.

Bryan: It's Fawn Creek, Madison. All I'd have to do is make a phone call. Or just drive around until I find your van.

Madison: Fine. Give me just a few minutes.

I stand from the sofa and untangle myself from the floral throw blanket I slept with last night. If you can even call it sleep. Unfortunately, I'm still not sleeping much at all when the girls are gone. Instead, I doze in and out of consciousness all night, and spend my days trying my best to survive on coffee and Diet Dr. Pepper instead. Quickly, I throw on a pair of sweatpants with the long T-shirt that I wore to bed. I slide on my slippers and a hoodie before making my way outside.

The frosty morning air sends a shiver straight to my bones and causes my teeth to chatter. If it's already this cold, I can only imagine what next week will feel like when the cold front hits. Even the old forgotten concrete porch goose at my neighbors house looks like she is shivering in the wind. She's still wearing her Christmas dress although it's March. Her red velvet dress almost appears to be covered in frost.

Of course, by the end of the weekend, she will be thawed. It's going to be seventy degrees. That's Kansas weather for you.

I climb into the van and close the driver's side door, to block myself from the bitter Kansas air. My finger locates the push button and again, like last night, I'm met with nothing. I let out a groan. I don't want to bother Bryan. He's in town for the weekend to see his family and get settled into his new house. I'm sure he has much better things to do than to fix the minivan of the single mom he had a one-night stand with in Mexico. However, I don't have a lot of other choices.

Disappointed, I climb out of my van and make my way back towards the house. As I walk inside, I hug my arms, trying to warm back up as quickly as possible and try to come up with a better solution than Bryan.

I could call my dad. Of course, if I do, then Bryan is going to be pissed at me for having someone else take care of it when he is willing to help.

Ben always took care of things like this. Most of the time, if something was broken, he could fix it. And if he couldn't, he would find someone who could. I never had to call a plumber or an electrician or anyone, for that matter. I only took my van to Fawn Creek Auto for oil changes because he wanted to support his friends' business. Of course, Ben's the last person I'm going to call on today, though. Yes, I'm sure he'd do it, but

I don't want him to have the satisfaction of having me run to him for help. I don't need him, but I do need some kind of help.

And we won't even bring up Jonathan. That's just as bad as letting Ben help me. Maybe even worse, to be honest.

Perhaps Bryan isn't a terrible choice after all. He's willing to help. He's a nice guy, and he just wants me to be safe. Besides, just because he's working on my car, that doesn't mean we are going to cross the line. We're both adults and I'm sure we can control ourselves, right?

I pick up my phone and fire off a message to Bryan.

Madison: No dice. It's not starting again.

Bryan: Ok, I am 95% sure it's your alternator. I'm going to run by the parts store and then come over and jump your van so we can get it into my shop. I can leave my truck at your place if you want me to or you can follow me to mine. Your choice.

I read the message and frown. If I let him leave his truck here, I can only imagine the rumors that would make way through town by the end of the day. Fawn Creek is a great place, but it's still a small town, and it doesn't take long for the rumors and speculation to make their way through the grapevine. I can only imagine how Ben would react. Not that he has the right to say anything at all to me about who is parked in my driveway. He lost that right when he got another woman pregnant.

At least at Bryan's house, my van will be in his shop and no one would see us, anyway. He lives outside of town, away from the main highway and out of the sight of the public.

Madison: I'll follow you to your house. I have nothing going

on today, anyway.

It's not a lie. I have a book that I bought from Tyler's bookstore and I've been trying to find the time to read it, anyway.

Bryan: It won't take long. I don't have a waiting area set up at the shop yet, but my house is ready and my furniture arrived this week. You can hang out in there.

Madison: Sounds good. I'll be ready. I'll send you my address.

Now, can I control myself when I'm alone with him all day?

* * *

Bryan unlocks the front door to his new house and pushes it open while I follow behind, taking it all in.

"I know it's not much. But it's home." He says with a grin, obviously proud of what he has created for himself.

"Whatever. It's beautiful." I say with a shake of my head.

I make my way through the space, admiring Bryan's pristine new home. Nothing about this place feels like a manufactured home, and I would have never guessed that it was if he hadn't told me. The white walls and dark floors give off a modern feeling that I wasn't expecting to find. The kitchen takes my breath away with the massive number of cabinets and a large island centered in the middle. Just the right size of a place to entertain a large family for years.

"How many bedrooms is it?" I ask, peering down a hallway, and counting the open doorways.

"Four beds, and two baths."

"That's a lot of space for one guy." I say, leading myself through the property on a self-guided tour.

Bryan pauses, as though he's trying to think of how to respond. "Well, maybe I won't be here alone forever." He answers slyly, his eyes resting on my lips a little longer than I am prepared for. Suddenly, standing in his bedroom, just feet from his king size bed, feels very real and very dangerous to me. I start to panic. We need to get back to the matter at hand.

"So, you think it's the alternator, huh?" I change the subject, taking a step back before leading him to the living room.

"Pretty sure." He confirms, following my lead. "It won't take me long to get it done. Make yourself comfortable." He says, pointing to the couch. "Sorry, I don't have cable or internet yet, but the cabinet next to the TV is full of movies."

I wave him off and pull my book from my purse. "No need. I have a book and any chance I can get for some uninterrupted reading time, I will take. Any idea what I'll owe you? I have some cash on me or I can cash app you."

Bryan snickers and runs his hand along his beard. "You aren't paying me."

"Yes, I am." I argue. "I can pay for my vehicle to be fixed."

"Nope, I'm doing this for you. Not to make money. I have plenty of spare time today and I would feel better knowing you will be safe on the road. Besides, then you can tell all your friends that I fixed your van and that will help me build up a customer base when I am fully back home."

"You need to at least let me pay for parts." I insist. "Alternators aren't cheap."

"Fine." He settles, shaking his head. "I'll be in the shop if you need me." He says, picking up the keys and making his way outside before I can argue.

I settle into his couch and open my book. Hopefully, he will be done quick, and I get out of here before I make a bad decision.

Chapter 13

The sound of running water causes me to stir. I open my eyes and look around the room, trying to make sense of where I am. It doesn't take me long to remember that I'm at Bryan's house, on his couch, with my open book laying on my chest. The last thing I remember was closing my eyes just for a second.

"Hey, sorry. I didn't mean to wake you." Bryan's voice booms from the kitchen. "I was just washing up."

I sit up fully on the sofa and rub my eyes. "It's fine. Sorry about that. I guess I dozed off reading. Hopefully, I didn't talk in my sleep or snore." I add.

"Not that I heard," Bryan assures me. "You were out pretty hard, though."

"Yeah, I didn't sleep well last night." I admit. "I don't sleep well at all when the girls are gone. You'd think by now I'd be more used to it, but so far, no luck."

"Well, it's a lot to get used to, I'm sure." Bryan says, sitting down on the sofa next to me.

He's just close enough that we could touch, but far enough away that we don't.

"Your van is done. It's starting every time now, so you should be good. I left it parked in the shop so it can stay warm until you leave. I changed the oil while I was at it. And aired up one of your tires. I won't even ask when the last time you took it in for an inspection."

"Thank you. You really didn't have to do all that. What do I owe you?"

He shakes his head. "I'll figure it out later. I'm going to return the old alternator to the store and they will give me a core deposit back. Then we can square away."

I eye him suspiciously. "You're never going to give me a price, are you?"

"Probably not." He confirms with a laugh. "Listen, I'm not worried about it. I just want to know that you are going to be taken care of when I'm not here. That's all the payment I need. My peace of mind is definitely worth enough."

"Why are you so worried about me?" I challenge him. "I'm not your problem, remember?"

Bryan lets out a heavy sigh and turns to face me. "Oh, but you are. You've been my problem since the day we met, Madison. Since the day your daughter fell in the street at the Christmas festival. And don't get me started on Mexico."

Just the mention of Mexico sends chills down my spine and immediately takes me back to that night. It was the night of Avery's wedding. I had a few more drinks than I had allowed myself to have throughout the entire trip. Our crew went to the nightclub at the resort and things got carried away. Bryan and I were dancing, and we were both getting a little hungry. We told everyone we were leaving to find something to eat. But all the on-site restaurants were closed, so we went back to his room to order room service. Standing on the balcony, waiting for our fries, I did something I had never done before. I made a move. I kissed him. And he kissed me back. And it just kept going. What started as a make-out session on the balcony escalated

105

quickly. The next thing I knew, we were moving to the bed and clothes were flung all over the place. And we woke up the next morning without ever eating our food from room service.

He kept asking, "Are you sure you want to do this?" and I kept telling him "Yes". And I really wanted it. I wanted him and his lips on mine and his hands in my hair, but also, I wanted to fall asleep on his chest. So, we did it all. As much as I want to regret what happened, I don't. He made me feel seen and wanted and sexy and, most importantly, safe. Falling asleep in his arms was the most secure I'd felt in over a year. I want that again. I want that every day if we are being honest. But... he's Avery's brother.

"What's going on in that pretty head of yours?" Bryan asks, scooting in closer to me and picking up my hand.

"Mexico."

His face softens and his eyes search mine. "I think about Mexico all the time." He confesses. "Madi, I'd give anything to go back there. To that night. Hell, to that entire week. I've never felt as connected to anyone as I felt to you. Not even close. And I haven't been able to shake you since we got back."

I stare down at my lap. Where his hand is still resting on mine. "Me too." I admit.

Bryan lets out a heavy sigh. "Then why are you pushing back so hard? Isn't it obvious that we belong together?"

I shake my head. "But, your sister..." I argue, but Bryan stops me.

He leans in close and gently tilts back my head. "No more excuses, Madison." He says, before crashing his lips into mine.

Before I know what's happening, his hands are in my hair and his lips are on my neck and every bit of my rational thinking goes out the window. It isn't long before the kisses go from soft and gentle to hungry and desperate. My body immediately is drawn to his and suddenly I'm in his lap, feeling his strong, callused hands under the hem of my shirt.

After several minutes, I pull back, resting my forehead on his in order to catch a breath.

"Do you want to move this to the bedroom?" He asks, not moving his eyes from mine.

I nod, unable to respond with words. Knowing if I even open my mouth, I'll appear too eager.

With that, he wraps his arms around my body, cradling me to him, and carries me off to his bed.

* * *

Bryan lets out a heavy breath and falls in place next to me before leaning over to kiss the side of my head. "That was...." He begins, only to be interrupted by the sound of his doorbell ringing through the house.

My eyes widen. Who could be ringing his doorbell? Who even knows he is here? "Are you expecting someone?"

He shakes his head. "Nope, not that I know of. Stay here, I'll get rid of them. Don't move."

Bryan climbs from the bed and works to redress himself before exiting the room. I lay under the covers, craning my neck as though it will help me determine who is here, interrupting our moment. Just then, a familiar voice carries through the house.

Avery.

I jump from the bed and redress myself.

"I'm here for my tour." Avery's muffled voice says through

the closed bedroom door.

"Well, you could have called first." Bryan retorts.

Shit. Shit. Shit.

How did this happen? I told myself nothing would happen with Bryan and then I let my guard down in a moment of weakness, only to put myself in this situation. Avery's going to catch me half naked in her brother's bedroom, and then our entire friendship is going to be tainted. Then, when Bryan and I break up, she's going to pull Juliet from my daycare because she will hate me and have to take her brother's side. I'm not only going to lose an income but also lose one of my kids that I've had for five days a week since she was six weeks old. I can't believe I was such an idiot. Again.

Once I'm fully dressed, I make a beeline for the closet door in search of a place to hide. I make it inside, just in time.

"Avery, wait." I hear Bryan's voice in a panicked tone as they both enter the attached bedroom.

"Geez you slob. I thought you military guys were trained to make the bed when you wake up in the morning. It looks like you've been rolling around in a pile of sheets for two days."

"Sorry, Mom." Bryan mutters, his voice sounding obviously confused about the fact that I'm not in the room.

"Oh, what's in here?" Avery asks, her voice growing louder, obviously standing just outside the closet door.

I move to the back of the closet and hide myself the best I can behind the few things Bryan has moved in and hung up. Luckily, a pile of boxes is in place for me to hide myself.

"Just a closet." Bryan's voice booms defensively. "Nothing to see."

"Oh, let me see it! You know I love a good closet."

"No. I'll give you a full tour once I get everything moved

in. It's a mess right now." Bryan insists, however Avery is relentless.

The closet door flings open and I hold my breath, hiding among the hanging clothing and piles of boxes.

"Nice. Very spacious." Avery says before closing the door. "That wasn't so hard, was it?"

I stand frozen in my hiding place, waiting for her to disappear, but the door flings open once again. "Madison, you can come out of the closet now."

I pause, remaining in my hiding place. Maybe if I don't respond, she will think she's wrong. How does she even know it's me?

"Madison." Avery repeats. "I can see your feet. You can stop hiding now."

I lean out from behind the pile of boxes and make eye contact with her. "Oh, hi," I reply, trying to sound casual. "I didn't know you were here."

Avery rolls her eyes. "Then why are you hiding in my brother's closet?"

"Um...." I say, trying to think of something, anything I can say. "Just doing some organizing. I thought I'd help him get some unpacking done. It was a surprise."

Avery's not buying it. She crosses her arms in front of her chest and stares at me. "You know you are both consenting adults and I don't care who you sleep with, right?"

"Oh weird, I feel like I told you that's exactly how she would feel." Bryan snickers.

Bryan and Avery both turn to look at me with a raised brow. I almost want to laugh at the sight of the two of them. Never have I realized how much they look alike until today.

"I just didn't want you to be mad."

"Why did you think I would care if you were seeing my brother?" She asks.

"I don't know." I admit, stepping out of the closet and walking into Bryan's room, taking a seat at the foot of his bed. "It just seemed inappropriate. You're my friend and Juliet is one of my daycare kids. It just felt like it was a boundary that I shouldn't be crossing. Like, it's against girl code or something."

Avery shakes her head. "Madison, it's only against girl code if we are a couple of teenage girls and you are pretending to be my friend so you can come over and drool over my brother. We're adults. If you two want to be together, then I will not get in the way of that."

I frown. "Are you sure you're not upset?"

She moves to sit next to me. "Of course I'm not upset. Madison, you have been through hell and back in the last year. You deserve to be happy. And while my brother is a pain in the ass, I think he does, too. I couldn't imagine wanting him with anyone else. I love you. You're already like family to me. At least I don't have to put on a fake smile and pretend to like whatever girl he dates when he comes home. It honestly saves me a lot of steps."

At that, I let out a relieved chuckle. "But what if it doesn't work out with him? You'll hate me."

"You need to give me more credit than that." She says, raising a brow. "I could never hate you. You are one of my best friends. Honestly, I'd probably disown him before I gave up on you." She adds, gently elbowing me.

I crack a small smile and pause to think. "Wait. How did you know I was here and know to come looking for me? My van is in the shop."

Avery laughs. "I saw your book on the coffee table. I may not know my brother well, but I highly doubt he reads romance novels."

Bryan snickers. "Now that, I can confirm."

I take a deep breath and look at both my friend and her brother. "Well, I have to admit. I think it's a relief to have this out in the open."

"The only one you were fooling was yourself, friend." Avery grins, standing from her seat. "I've known all about this since we landed in Mexico. I'm just glad you are ready to admit it. So, I'll be expecting both of you at mom's tomorrow for lunch before Bryan heads back home."

I frown. "Isn't it a bit soon for a family get together?"

Bryan laughs. "Nope. We have the last two months to make up for." He says, grabbing my hand and pulling me from the bed. I crash into his chest, and he leans down to find my lips with his.

"Gross." Avery shakes her head. "At least let me leave before you two start playing catch up."

Chapter 14

"Madison, hi!" Julie says as she holds the screen door open for me to make my way into her house. I'm holding a container of cookies that I baked last night.

"You did not need to bring anything." She says, opening the lid to the container and peeking inside.

I wave her off. "Last night, I baked cookies to pass the time. I figured I'd bring some to share."

What I don't tell her is that even though I already know and love Bryan's family, the thought of coming over for their Sunday meal had me up all night. After Bryan and I finally parted ways around nine o'clock, I came home and tried to sleep. After an hour of laying on the couch, I finally gave up and ransacked my kitchen for something to bake.

"I hope you like lemon cookies. Warmer weather always makes me want lemon-flavored things." I confess.

"I love lemon and so does Bryan." She says with a wink. "I love your outfit, too."

I glance down at my clothes that I almost didn't put on today, before following her into the kitchen. I'm wearing the hot pink romper I picked up from Myrtles and a pair of white strappy sandals. It's almost spring here in Fawn Creek and thanks to the bipolar Kansas weather, we are having an unseasonably warm day. Since I wanted to look nice, it seemed like the perfect chance to wear it. "Thank you. It's new. I know it's a little extra, but..."

Julie holds up a hand to stop me from speaking. "Absolutely not. It is not extra. It's perfect, and it looks so good on you. Never apologize for wearing what makes you happy."

I nod. "You're right. I love it and I feel super cute, but also, it's a little intimidating. I haven't worn something like this since..."

"Since before you became a mom?"

I nod. "Since before I became a mom."

Julie smiles softly. "You know what this means? This means you are getting your pink back."

I look down at my outfit once again and back at her with what I'm sure is an obvious look of confusion on my face. "Huh?"

"Just like a flamingo." Julie explains. "The reason flamingos have that pink color is that the pigmentation comes from the nutrients in the foods that they eat. When they have babies, they pass all those nutrients, including the pigments, off to their babies. This results in causing the mothers' colors to fade and they become pale looking. However, once the babies grow and feed themselves, the moms have time to replenish their own bodies. And their pink comes back. Humans are the same way. We give so much to our kids, physically, mentally, emotionally. We love them so much, but it is a lot of work and it's easy to lose parts of ourselves. When you're deep in the trenches of motherhood, it's easy to let it become your entire personality. However, eventually, our babies grow up and don't need us twenty-four-seven anymore. Then, little by little, we find ourselves again. And we get our pink back, too."

I pause, looking down at my shoes while I ponder what she

just said. "So, this is normal? This feeling like I'm lost and have no idea who I am anymore?"

"Oh, honey." Julie says, as she pulls me into a hug. "Of course, it's normal. But you're getting yourself back. Little by little. I can see it. You're coming out the other side of this big ole mess you've been in and I love seeing you come back to life."

"Thank you. Me too." I agree with a smile.

"Also, I am so glad you and Bryan are seeing each other." She adds with a wide smile. "I couldn't have picked a better girl for him to date."

I nod. "He's great. I'm glad we are giving it a try, too."

"He is. I'm glad to see him happy. And you deserve it, too. I've been hoping for this ever since we were in Mexico for Avery's wedding." She confesses. "I saw the way you two hit it off. I knew you had to be more than just friends."

"Hey, there you are," Avery says, saving me from the awkward exchange. "We're all out here." She adds, motioning towards the backyard. "Come say hi."

I nod and excuse myself before following Avery through the patio door. "Thank you." I whisper as we make it outside. "It was getting weird in there." I admit, just as I look up to see who else is in the yard. I pause and hold my hand up to wave to Andrew, Derek, Bryan and Tyler as they stand around the propane grill in Julie's backyard.

"I thought this was a family thing." I whisper.

"We're all family here." Avery chuckles.

"Nothing like hard launching a new relationship with everyone I know." I grumble.

"Might as well rip off the band-aid." Avery says with a grin.

"Hey, there you are." Bryan makes his way towards me with

no hesitation. Pausing only when he stops in front of me and lightly kisses my lips in front of our entire friend group.

I turn and brace myself to see the reactions from Derek, Tyler, and Andrew, but no one says a word.

"If you're waiting for us to react, you're too late. Bryan already told us. And we are not at all surprised." Tyler says with a wink. "We just wish you would have done this in Mexico and saved us all a lot of time."

I raise a brow. "So what.. all of you knew we liked each other?"

"No, we knew you two hooked up in Mexico." Tyler says.

I can feel the color drain from my face.

"Did you think we were stupid? We saw the way you two looked at each other. And the way you were dancing in the nightclub. Then you told us you were leaving because you were hungry? We're not delusional enough to think that was innocent."

"You were hungry for something alright." Bryan laughs, his face turning beet red.

I let out a groan. I guess I'm not as sneaky as I thought I was.

"Hey, at least we didn't give you any crap about it. We just let you pretend you weren't interested. Even after Sierra told us she caught you sneaking back to your room during your walk of shame the morning after the wedding." Avery shrugs.

"You knew?" I ask, eyes darting between my group of friends.

"Yes, of course we knew. But it wasn't our business. Madi, we just want you to be happy. And if my brother is the one who makes you happy, then that's even better." Avery smiles softly.

"Okay, that's enough mushy crap." Andrew says, piling one

final piece of grilled chicken onto a cooking sheet. "Let's eat."

* * *

Bryan leans forward to kiss me through his truck window one more time before letting out a loud groan. "I hate that I have to leave and head back home tonight." He says, reaching out and squeezing my hand.

I nod. "Me too. When do you think you'll be home again?"

"Couple weeks, maybe? I'm not sure."

I offer him a half smile. "That's okay. Only a couple more months and then you'll be here all the time."

"And you'll be sick of me." He says with a laugh.

"I highly doubt it." I say, standing on the side step of his pickup to kiss him one more time. Just then, headlights shine into his truck, as my ex-husband drives up and parks in my driveway.

"Shit. That's my kids. I better go." I trail off. While we might have hard launched our relationship to our friends today, I'm not really ready to do the same with my kids. I'd really like to date him for at least a few weeks before springing the news on them.

"I totally get it. I'll text you when I get home. Bye, Freckles." He says with a smile as I back away from the truck and he pulls off from the curb.

I walk towards the driveway to meet the kids. Pausing to hug each of them before leading them towards the house.

"Who was that?" Kenzi asks, pointing towards Bryan's truck.

"Um... a friend of mine." I offer, as I let her pass me and disappear into the house.

"Really?" Ben asks, shaking his head as he watches the path the black pickup took. "Bryan Thompson?"

I scoff and turn to face Ben. "Yes, Bryan Thompson. What's wrong with that?"

"Well, nothing if you like guys that are too old for you. What is he, 40?"

"No, he's 38." I answer matter-of-factly. "And who are you, my dad?"

"That's basically the same age." Ben mutters. "Besides, isn't he in the military? He doesn't even live here."

"He's retiring and will move home in a couple of months." I explain.

Ben laughs. "Did you really just say that your boyfriend is retired? Doesn't that sound weird to you?"

"Why are you being so mean about this?" I ask.

Ben pauses and looks at me with a solemn expression. "Madi, I'm sorry. I just don't want you to get hurt. Or for you to move on to a rebound guy too fast."

I scoff. "How kind of you to be so worried about protecting my feelings suddenly."

Ben throws his hands in the air. "See? That's what I'm saying? You obviously aren't over us yet. It's too soon for you to move on. Madison, you aren't ready. You aren't even yourself anymore. You cut your hair and painted your house, and what are you wearing?" He asks, pointing at my outfit. "What happened to you? You've changed."

"You're right, Ben." I say, with a nod. "I have changed. And these changes are for the better. I am finally doing the things that make me happy instead of worrying constantly about what you'll think. Look, I'm sorry you found this way that I'm seeing someone, but that's all I'm sorry for. Don't try to make me feel guilty for taking charge of my life. You don't get to control me or my feelings anymore. It's time for you to leave, I think."

I turn on my heel and storm into the house, closing the door behind me. Ben is the last person who's going to make me feel bad about finding happiness.

Chapter 15

BEEP, BEEP, BEEP.

The sound of my alarm clock screaming in the darkness jolts me awake. I roll over and silence the alarm before looking at my notifications. The very first one on my screen is from Bryan.

Bryan: Good morning, beautiful. I hope you have a good day.

I read the text and fire one off back to him.

Madison: Morning. I hope you slept good.
Bryan: I'll sleep better when I'm back there with you.
Madison: Not much longer!

It's been three days since Bryan headed back home and we officially started our long distance relationship. The past few days have been full of text exchanges throughout the day and quiet phone calls after the girls go to sleep at night. But, it's been nice. Not that I have much experience dating, but I have to admit the long distance relationship has felt like less pressure. We text, we talk on the phone, but I don't have to stress about making plans and seeing each other every minute. Especially when I'm already so busy with the girls. Hopefully, we will continue to get along just as well when we are living in the same state.

Bryan: It'll be here before we know it. I'm ready. The guys are going out to the new house to install my storm shelter today and then my house will be ready. All that will be left is finishing this contract.

Madison: Oh, I'm jealous. I'd love to have a shelter here. Especially while I have other people's kids in my care.

Bryan: What do you do when there's a storm?

Madison: We load up in my van and make a beeline for the community storm shelter at the church.

Bryan: That seems stressful.

Madison: It's not ideal, but it's better than ducking into the bathtub with a house full of toddlers. If money was no object, I'd have a safe room installed in my garage, but they aren't cheap. And this has worked out for me so far.

Bryan: I don't like that, Freckles.

Madison: It is what it is. I better go get ready before I have to get the girls up. Have a good day. Hey, what's your plan for dinner tonight?

Bryan: Nothing. Probably a box of Hamburger Helper in front of the TV.

Madison: How about a FaceTime date for dinner? My kids will be gone, and this is my one quiet night this week.

Bryan: You want to eat on FaceTime?

Madison: Yeah. Why not? So, say 6:30 tonight? Have your dinner ready to eat.

Bryan: It's a date.

* * *

"Goodnight, friends." I say as I click off the light switch next to the front door, and tiptoe towards the sofa. I turn on our lullaby playlist and get cozy to read my latest romance novel while the kids rest.

Today we've been blessed with another beautiful day This is what we in Kansas call Fake Spring. Fake Spring comes in quickly when we least expect it after spending weeks on end dealing with snow, sleet and a wind chill that hurts your face when you step outside. Suddenly, you wake up one day and you don't need a coat or gloves to check the mail. A light jacket is all you need, and sometimes that is even too much. We Kansans eat this crap up.

We spend time outside as though we've been confined to the inside for months on end. We sit in the sun and point our faces to the light and enjoy every single second that we can. And we forget about when the weather just tried to freeze us to death. Or the fact that a cold front will be here this week.

Today, the kids and I took full advantage of Fake Spring. After breakfast, we put the school aged kids on the bus, did circle time and then headed to the backyard.

We sat on the patio while I read the kids their stories. Then, we did music and movement by going on a bear hunt and having an outdoor dance party.

We got out the sensory table and filled it with sand, not caring how much we dropped on the ground while we made sand castles.

And we stayed outside until we had no other choice than to go in so I could make lunch.

Now lunch has been consumed, and my little besties are snuggled under their blankets on the floor. And I am thankful for a break to read my book while they rest.

"Miss Madi?" The voice of Carson, a three-year-old boy, cuts through the music just as I'm getting comfortable.

"Yes?"

"Can you pat my back?" He asks, turning to look at me with soft eyes.

Carson is one of my newest kids and one that I took in merely because I needed more income when I found out that my daycare was going to have to support me full time. What I wasn't expecting was for this kid to be one of the sweetest kiddos I've ever watched.

"Of course, buddy." I say, climbing down from the sofa and taking a seat next to him on the floor. Dutifully, Carson rolls over to lie on his stomach and I start our new routine of gently patting his back just between his shoulder blades. His father, a single dad, had warned me that this might be the norm for him, at least here in the beginning. Previously, Carson had been primarily watched by Eric's mom, ever since Carson's mom gave birth to him and then dutifully decided she didn't want to be a mom after all. She left Carson with Eric for his weekend visitation and then just never picked him up again.

I admit, when Eric told me the story, it broke my heart. Who could ever look down at their baby and just decide to leave? Even if I didn't need the income, I couldn't have turned down bringing this sweet kid into my home. Hopefully, while I know I'll never replace his mom, I hope I can show him love while he's here.

I never pictured myself running a daycare center in my house. Honestly, when I was younger, I didn't know what I wanted to be. Until the day I gave birth to Kate. As soon as I looked at her, I knew in my heart that the most important job I could ever have was raising my babies. Now, looking around the room at all my snoozing kiddos, I can't help but think maybe I really was put on this Earth to be their safe space.

Maybe the real me wasn't that long gone after all.

* * *

"Hi!" I say as Bryan answers the FaceTime call and his face fills the screen.

"Hey." He replies. He takes a seat at his table, with a plate of food sitting in front of him.

"Well, what are you having tonight?"

"Hamburger Helper of course." He laughs. "It's difficult to cook for just one person. What about you?"

I look down at my plate. "I'm having leftovers from what I cooked for the kids for lunch today. So, chicken alfredo, salad, green beans and garlic bread."

"I'm jealous." Bryan admits.

"Well, if I was just cooking for myself, I would either be eating a ham and cheese sandwich or picking up something from one of the restaurants in town. I have this daycare food thing down to a science. Lunch is the one time a day that I cook an actual meal. Then, the kids and I use the leftovers for dinner. Usually after a full day of entertaining tiny people, I am too tired to stand at the stove and cook dinner."

"Makes sense." He replies, taking a quick bite of his meal. Once he finishes chewing, he pauses to look at the screen. "So, did you always want to run a daycare?"

I shake my head. "No. Honestly, growing up, I wasn't sure what I wanted to do. I knew I wanted to be a mom, but that was it. I only started watching kids because Kate's daycare closed down and we didn't have any other options in town."

"Do you like it?"

"I love it." I admit. "At first, it was a little intimidating to get a routine figured out. I had never worked in a daycare center, and I don't have any kind of formal education in Early Childhood Development. Luckily, my neighbor, Carolyn, used to be a childcare center director, so she helped me every step of the way. I don't think I would enjoy what I do so much if it wasn't for her. Now, I can't see myself doing anything else."

"So, do you think you'll ever open a bigger daycare? It sounds like Fawn Creek doesn't have a lot of child care options. Have you thought about opening a center like your neighbor used to work at?"

I shake my head. "No, not really. More than one person has suggested that I go back to school to get a teaching degree or maybe open a daycare center in town. No one seems to understand that none of that is my dream. I'm just content with what I'm doing now. Is that strange?"

Bryan shakes his head. "No, not at all."

I let out a sigh of relief. "Good. I just feel like there's a lot of pressure on women to do more with their lives. I mean, look at my friends. Tyler owns a bookstore, Avery has a great career, plus she's going to open her boutique and she does her social media thing. Ava has her real estate stuff and Sierra has her own salon. I feel like I should want more. Maybe I should want to open my own child care center and be the director. But, I don't want to. The whole 'boss babe' thing isn't for me. I want to teach a few kids to share and take turns. I want to play with Playdough, feed them new things, and read to them. I'm not trying to change the world. I just wanna do my small part for Fawn Creek."

Bryan, who has put his fork down on his plate and given me his full attention through my rant, smiles softly. "Madison, I think you are changing the world right where you are. Those kids are lucky to have you, and I am, too. Don't ever feel like you need to do more than you are right now."

* * *

It's Thursday evening and I'm sitting at the kitchen table sanitizing our wooden blocks when the doorbell rings. I quickly make my way to the door and open to find Avery on the other side.

"Hey, come on in." I say, holding the door open for her.

She walks in and immediately is tackled by an awaiting Juliet.

"Mommy!" Juliet squeals as Avery bends down to pick her up.

"You're in a good mood today! Did you have a good day?" Avery asks.

Juliet responds with an excited head nod.

Avery kisses the side of Juliet's head. "Good. I'm glad. Go get your shoes and we will head home." She tells her daughter, before putting her on the floor and turning to face me, lowering her voice. "Hey, keep an eye on the weather. It's supposed to get kind of nasty tonight."

I frown. "Please tell me you're kidding. I'm not ready for tornado season yet." I groan.

"Me neither, but it's here." She huffs. "Hopefully, it'll fall apart before it gets here, but Derek is adamant that it's going to be bad. Just stay alert. The church will be open if you need to go."

I frown and stand up from the table. "Guess I'll pack my go bag and be on standby. Thanks for the heads up."

"Anytime."

Chapter 16

"The tornado watch for Montgomery County, Kansas, has expired." The meteorologist reports from my living room TV.

"Thank God." I mutter, picking up the remote and turning off the news broadcast. It's been a long evening of doing nothing but worrying about the weather, and thankfully nothing came out of it.

I reach over and pick up my phone to check the time. Then, I fire off a text to Bryan letting him know we are in the clear. He and I have been texting basically nonstop tonight, both watching the storm cell that was slowly making its way to Fawn Creek.

Because of the uncertainty of the storms, I already had the girls run through most of their bedtime routine. Showers were taken, shoes set out by my emergency backpack, and clothes set out for tomorrow.

"Girls! It's time to brush your teeth and get ready for bed!" I call out to them.

I brace myself, waiting for an argument to begin, but luckily they do as they are told, with only a couple of moans and groans.

Once the girls are tucked into bed, I make my way through the house, finishing up my evening chores to get ready for tomorrow. I start the dishwasher and the dryer. I pick up the house and make sure the meat is thawed for tomorrow. Then I take a long, hot shower to prepare for my own bedtime.

Just as I finish lathering up my hair, my phone rings on the counter. I stick my soapy head out of the shower and I'm surprised to see the call is coming from Bryan.

Quickly, I put my head under the showerhead and get my shampoo out before stepping away from the water stream. I'm about to call him back when the phone rings again.

"Hello?"

"Madison, are you taking cover?" Bryan asks breathlessly.

Confused, I pause. Still standing naked in my bathroom, with water dripping on the surrounding floor. "No. The watch expired. I'm in the shower."

"You need to get out of the shower and get into shelter. There's a tornado heading right for Fawn Creek. It'll be hitting the ground in fifteen minutes."

"What? No. This is crazy." I argue, but quickly shut off the water. The sound of the city tornado siren can be heard faintly off in the distance as soon as the water is turned off. I throw the phone on the counter, now on speakerphone, and throw on my clothes and wrap my hair up in a messy bun.

"It came out of nowhere. Even the weatherman was shocked to see it."

"Well, thank God you were still watching. When the weatherman said we were safe, I shut it off and moved on with my life." I say, making my way through the house to gather up the girls. "The siren is going off, but I guess I couldn't hear it over the shower. Okay, I'm going to go so I can get the girls out the door. Thank you."

"You're welcome. And Madison, be careful, okay?"

"I will." I promise, before disconnecting the call and opening

Kate's bedroom door. "Hey Sister, wake up. We have to go to the church."

"Why?" Kate groans. "I thought the storm was over."

"Me too." I admit. "But one popped back up. Get your shoes on, please, while I get your sister." Without a pause, I push into Kenzi's room. "Kenzi, wake up, baby. We have to go to the church."

Kenzi's eyes fly open. "Is it a tornado? Is our house going to get sucked up?"

"No, we are going to be okay and our house will too, but we need to get to the church just in case." I tell her, as a now awake and grumpy looking Kate stands in the hall, waiting for us.

"Shoes on, let's roll." I tell Kenzi.

Within minutes, the girls and I are making our way outside, and running through a light rain across the yard into my awaiting van. I buckle in Kenzi while Kate works on her own belt in her booster seat.

Once inside, we make the three-minute drive across town to the Methodist church, with my heart pounding. I know Bryan said we had time. I know we will be okay, but the whirl of the siren and the green tinted sky, a sky that appears much lighter than it should be at this time of night, has my nerves shot. Please God, don't let anything happen to my babies. Keep my town safe.

We locate a parking spot at the church and I jump out of the driver's seat, nearly at the same time that I shut off the ignition. I open the driver's side sliding door and lean in to unbuckle Kenzi, faster than I've ever done before. As she climbs out of the van, I catch a glimpse of the sky.

Immediately, I'm full of regret. A giant wall cloud is building and hanging out just over the church parking lot. These are the types of clouds that indicate a tornado is coming. This really could take our entire town out. And there's nothing we can do but hunker down and pray.

I grab each girl by one hand and we make a mad dash across the parking lot, trying to avoid puddles but ultimately failing.

Cody, Sierra's husband, is standing at the door helping everyone get inside. He offers me a soft smile as I thank him and we make our way into the church. We turn towards the safe room in the basement and I pause in the doorway, taking in the sight in front of me.

I've been in this basement many times throughout the years. This is where we had our Girl Scout meetings and where I went to preschool. This is where families gather after funerals, where our excited grandmothers hosted their baby showers, and where we host ours still today. There have been so many emotions in this room, but tonight the fear and anxiety are apparent. Not only is the room full of fear, but it's full of at least half of the community of Fawn Creek. From newborn babies to senior citizens, every chair is filled with a person wearing the same weary expression. The same fear filling their mind. Tornadoes are nothing to mess around with. We've seen what they can do, and so far we've been lucky enough to not be devastated by one ourselves. Hopefully, that luck continues.

I lock eyes with Ava and make my way towards her, taking a seat on the floor at her side. Kate and Kenzi take turns hugging Piper, and the three girls share a stack of books that Piper has pulled from her Spiderman backpack. I pull my phone from my pocket and fire off a text to Bryan to let him know we made it. Then, I text my parents to make sure they are sheltering too. My mom confirms almost immediately that they are in the neighbor's basement.

"You okay?" Ava asks. She looks as tired as I feel with her sleek black hair up in a messy bun.

I nod, lying to her. I have to keep a strong front in case the girls notice.

"I'm glad you're here. I was just about to call you when I saw you walk through the door." She says. "I feel like there are so many people I need to check on all at once. Maybe I should make a tornado group chat." She says.

"Bryan called and interrupted my shower. The news said we were clear, so I was just going on with my life as usual, getting ready for bed. What if I hadn't heard the siren? My phone hasn't even gone off telling me to take shelter yet."

She shakes her head. "I bet you would have heard the siren eventually. But you might not have had time to get here. I'm glad you did. That was nice of him to watch out for you."

"It was." I agree, turning towards her. "I'm not good at this weather stuff. Ben used to watch it for me and tell me when I needed to take shelter." Come to think of it, I'm surprised he didn't text me either. Ben has been nothing but short with me since finding out that I was dating Bryan. But, even if he is mad at me, shouldn't he at least send me a text and make sure his kids are okay? I fire off a text to him. He may not be worried about us taking shelter, but I don't want anything to happen to him. For my girl's sake.

"Carson!" Kenzi's voice cuts through the crowd as the little boy from my daycare runs across the basement and takes a seat next to the girls.

I tell Carson hi and then turn to see his dad making his way towards us. "Hey, Eric. This is Ava, Piper's mom." I say, motioning towards her.

"Nice to meet you." He says with a smile. "Sorry, I hope he

didn't interrupt anything." He goes on, motioning to Carson. "Carson was just excited to see his friends. He thinks we're doing something fun and exciting here."

"He's fine." I wave Jason off. "This is a stressful time, so he might as well have friends to hang out with. It'll be good to keep his mind preoccupied while we wait it out."

"Absolutely. The more the merrier." Ava chimes in, flashing Eric the type of genuine smile that I'm not sure I've ever seen her share with anyone else.

"Thanks. I appreciate it for sure." He smiles back. "Hey, I'm going to go check in with my parents. They are just right over there." He points across the room. "Will he be okay until I get back?"

"Sure!" I confirm before Eric turns to walk away. "He's safe with us."

"He's cute." Ava whispers.

"He's single, too." I reply, wiggling my eyebrows. "I could fix you up."

"No, no, no." Ava laughs. "Just because you found a boy doesn't mean I need to."

"But you're the only single one in our group now. You have to. It's the law."

"Nope. I'm busy building a business. I don't need any distractions."

"I think you do." I say with a smirk. "He's a cute distraction, too. And such a nice guy. Plus, Carson is the sweetest little boy I've ever met."

Ava lets out a heavy sigh. "No, thank you." She groans just as Cody's voice breaks through the crowd as he stands in the basement's doorway.

"Okay folks. I just got the all clear. The weather event is

over. The cyclone fell apart just outside of town and there is no longer a threat. You can go home and go back to bed. Hopefully, we won't have to do this too many times for the rest of storm season. You never can tell with these things, though."

A round of applause breaks out throughout the room as Cody finishes his announcement. I check my watch.

"Just in time to go home and go straight to bed." I laugh. "I hope the rest of storm season isn't like this. Especially during the day. I hate having to drag all the kids down here."

Ava frowns. "I never even thought of that. I guess I've always come and got Piper when it's storming, when I should have been sticking around to help you."

I shake my head. "No, it's okay. A lot of people come and get their kids. Just sometimes they don't have any other choice."

Ava frowns. "You need a storm shelter at the house. That would help so much."

I nod. "Bryan and I talked about that, too. I don't know if I could manage getting a bunch of kids into an in ground shelter and the above ground ones are so expensive. There's no way I could swing that."

"I bet there are grants out there. And lucky for you, I just took a grant writing class. Let me do some research and see what I can find out for you."

"Really? That would be incredible."

She nods. "Yep. It wouldn't hurt to see what we can find." She says with a shrug as Eric makes his way back towards us.

"Hey, Carson. It's time to go, kiddo." He tells his son, before turning back to look at us. "Thanks for letting him hang out with you guys."

"But, I'm playing with my friends. I don't want to go home." Carson says with a pout, obviously not ready to interrupt his middle of the night play date.

"We will all see you in just a few hours at my house." I assure Carson. "But, for now, you need to go home and rest so you have the energy to play when you get there."

"Fine. Bye Kate. Bye Kenzi. Bye Piper." He says, still pouting as he makes his way towards his dad. He grabs Eric's hand and they make their way towards his awaiting grandparents. I turn to catch Ava watching Eric's every step.

"Do I suspect a small crush?" I ask, wiggling my eyebrows.

"No." Ava answers immediately. "I told you. I'm too busy building a life for myself to be worried about some dude. But he is nice to look at."

Chapter 17

"Good morning!" Avery calls out as she opens the front door to my house and steps inside.

"Morning." I groan in response as I stand at the counter separating plates of scrambled eggs for the kids.

"I have something for you, and it looks like you're going to need it." Avery says as she places Juliet on the floor and dashes back out the front door. She returns with a cold coffee in her hands. "Vanilla cold brew latte." She says as she hands it over to me. "I got it without ice, thinking maybe you'd want it for this afternoon, but it looks like you're going to need a jolt this morning instead."

I take the coffee from her. "Bless you, woman. Yes, I need this for sure. Truly, I think I could go for a coffee IV at this point. When we got home from the church last night, the girls were completely wired. They had gotten maybe a thirty-minute nap before we left to take shelter and that was apparently enough to energize them for hours."

"Same with Juliet. We ended up running down the street to my mom's house. She's a pretty popular lady since she's one of the few people in town with a storm cellar. But I think being with Grandma riled her up even more."

"I bet it did, but the church wouldn't have been any better."

I laugh. "Half of the town of Fawn Creek was there in their jammies last night. I assume the other half was holed up in the other church on the other side of town. I didn't even hear the siren go off. Your brother was watching the weather and called to tell me to take shelter."

Avery frowns. "That's concerning. Come to think of it, I usually get a notification on my phone, but I didn't get one at all."

"Same. Maybe it just popped up too quickly? Luckily, it wasn't worse than it was."

She frowns. "What if we hadn't been so lucky? I'm going to call Derek on the way to work. I wonder if that's something that the city of Fawn Creek can help with."

Ava and Piper walk through the door, stalling our conversation for a beat. We both turn to tell them hi and then I continue with my thoughts. "We could have people sign up for text alerts and then they can be alerted when there's an emergency like that. It shouldn't be too hard to organize. And who knows, that might save a life one day."

"Good idea. I'll ask him about that today." Avery says, yawning. "If I can stay awake that long. It's going to be a long tornado season."

"Speaking of that." Ava says, joining us in the kitchen after getting Piper settled. "I couldn't sleep last night when we got home, and I got to googling. There is a grant that you can apply for to help you get an above ground shelter put in your garage. The bad news is, it's only going to cover 75% of the cost, even if you get approved for it."

I frown. "So, I'd still need to come up with over two thousand dollars on my own. Honestly, I don't know if I could even swing that much."

"We can help!" Avery suggests. "I'm sure we can organize a few fundraisers and get you there in no time."

"Absolutely." Ava agrees. "I'll get your application done, and Avery, if you want to brainstorm a list of fundraisers?"

"On it." She agrees.

I look at my friends. "Girls, thank you. This already seems like a lot to take on."

Ava shrugs. "Hey, this is just as much for my kid, too. Tornadoes scare the hell out of me and knowing she has a safe place to take shelter while at your house is more than enough motivation for me to help."

"Agreed." Avery pipes up. "The peace of mind to keep our kids safe and to make it easier for you to do so will make it worth it. Let us know what we can do to help. We will make this happen one way or another."

* * *

"You made it!" My mom calls out to me as I make my way towards her and my dad at the baseball field.

I have my wagon loaded down with chairs , snacks, toys and blankets.

"You know it's just one game, right? You don't have to move in." Dad teases.

I let out a sigh. "I know, but keeping your grand kids entertained at a game is more work than you think."

"Oh honey, if it was too much, you could have stayed home and come next week while the girls are with Ben." Mom suggests.

I shake my head. "And miss Nathan's first varsity game?

Absolutely not. The girls have snacks and their Barbies. They will be just fine."

"Mom, can we go to the concession stand? I'm hungry." Kate begs, sticking out her bottom lip into a pout.

"No, we brought snacks with us." I answer.

"But they have better snacks." Kenzi chimes in, now joining her sister in the begging.

My dad stands from his folding chair. "Welp, we better go see what they have then." He tells my begging children. "Anyone else want anything?"

I shake my head. "I'm fine." I tell him as I finish setting up our folding chairs.

"Popcorn." Mom says with a smile as she hands him a twenty-dollar bill.

"Got it. We will be right back," Dad promises, before leading my girls away from us.

"You know, you guys are not helping me keep those girls from being spoiled." I say turning towards my mother."

"Spoiling them is our job, Madi. Those are our first and only grand babies and we love them."

"I know Mom. I just find it funny how you never had concession stand money when I was a kid, but it's no problem now." I say, offering her a wink so she knows I'm teasing.

"Hey! Can I sit with you guys?" A voice interrupts our conversation.

I look up to see a teenage girl with a camping chair slung over her shoulder standing beside me.

"Yes, of course!" My mom gushes before turning to me. "Avery, this is Becca, Nathan's girlfriend."

"Oh! Nice to meet you. I'm Avery, Nathan's sister. Sit wherever." I say, moving the girls' chairs so they are in front of me. "My kids will probably not sit down in their chairs the entire time they're here."

Becca unpacks her chair and places it next to me before making her way to the dugout to see my brother.

"She's cute." I say to my mom. "Do we like her?"

"We love her." Mom gushes. "She is the sweetest girl. She always helps me in the kitchen when she comes over and cleans up after herself. We lucked out with that one for sure."

"Good. I'm glad to see Nathan dating someone that's worth a crap." I confess.

Mom elbows me. "I can't believe how overprotective you still are of him."

I shake my head. "He was my first baby! You had him when I was eleven. I feel like I helped raise him."

"Well, you did a good job. He turned out to be a great kid." Mom smiles. "You all did."

I watch as Becca waves goodbye to Nathan and makes her way back over to us.

"So, Becca. Do you have any plans next week for Spring Break?" Mom asks when she returns.

Becca shakes her head. "No, I was going to find some kids to watch or something. I'm trying to save up for a car. But, I think I waited too late. Everyone seems to have things figured out already, or I'm asking the wrong people."

I pause and consider what she said for a second before turning to her. "You know, I could use some help. I run a home daycare and I'm constantly turning people away that need a sitter over Spring Break. If I had a helper, we could take on a few more kids for the week."

"Really?"

I nod. "Yeah, and if this goes well, I could probably use some help over the summer, too. If you're interested. They'd be pretty busy days, but I could make it worth it for you."

"I'd love to." Becca grins. "I love kids and I'm thinking I might go to school to get a teaching degree."

"Okay, give me your number. We will work out details tomorrow after I make some calls." I say, handing her my phone.

"Perfect! Thank you." She says as she enters herself as a contact. "I'm so excited."

"It'll be great." I assure her, just as I look up and see a familiar figure making his way towards us.

"Bryan, what are you doing here? I thought you were still at work?" I ask as he reaches me. He pulls his folding chair off his shoulder and gives me a quick peck on the cheek.

"I wanted to surprise you." He says. "I hope it's okay."

"Better than okay." I assure him, just as the girls and my dad make their way back to us.

"Bryan, hey," Dad says, shaking his hand. "Glad you could make it."

"Me too. I'm a sucker for a good baseball game," He admits, as Kenzi pauses at his side.

"Do I know you?" She asks. "I think I've seen you before."

Bryan looks at me and back at Kenzi. I haven't quite told the girls that we are dating, but I imagine once they go back to Ben's, they will find out. Even so, I want to ease into this discussion.

I look over and smile softly at Bryan. "Kenzi, Kate, this is my friend Bryan. He's Juliet's Uncle."

"I know you!" Kenzi squeals. "You took me to get a sucker and a band aid when I fell down meeting Santa."

Bryan lets out a chuckle and a nod. "Yep, that was me. I'm

surprised you remember that."

"I do. You were really nice." She informs him before turning to me and climbing into my lap. Kenzi wraps her arm around my neck before whispering in my ear. "I like him, mommy. He's nice. I hope you two are friends for a long time."

* * *

"Great job!" I tell my little brother Nathan as he makes his way over to us following the game. The Fawn Creek Prairie Dogs won against Wayside Warriors in a blowout game of 57-2. "You have worked hard since last year and it shows. I'm so proud of you."

Nathan puts his arm around Becca and kisses her cheek before answering. "Thanks for coming. It felt good to be back out there."

"You keep this up and colleges are going to be fighting over you to play college ball." Dad says, rubbing the top of Nathan's head like he did back when Nathan was just a kid playing peewee ball.

"I hope so." Nathan grins. "So, what's for dinner? I'm starving."

I give my brother a hug. "I am going to head home and feed my own kids. Good job again. Send me your game schedule and I'll make as many games as I can. I can't wait to watch you kick ass this year."

"Thanks, sis." Nathan blushes as I tell my parents goodbye and go to gather up the rest of my crew. Bryan, Kate and Kenzi are just behind where we had our chairs set up. They've been playing catch with a random softball for at least half an hour now.

"Are you three ready to go?" I ask, standing with my hands on my hips.

"Mom." Kate yells, running to me. "I need a baseball glove. I think I would be really good at baseball."

I pause and look at Bryan, who offers me a shrug. "She's got a good arm."

I nod. "Okay, we can get you a glove. And signups for coach pitch softball should start up soon. If that's something you want to try."

"Mom, can I play baseball, too?" Kenzi asks, standing up from the pile of dirt that she's playing in.

I nod. "I think you are old enough for tee ball if you want to try that."

"I do!" She squeals. "I want a pink bat and a pink glove and a pink hat."

I turn to look at Bryan. "Sounds like we are going to spend a lot of time at the fields this summer."

Chapter 18

"Mom! Kenzi is eating all the pepperoni!" Kate's voice carries into the laundry room as I crouch onto the floor, changing the laundry from the washer to the dryer.

"Kate, it's fine! There's plenty!" I call back.

We were supposed to be having a nice quiet evening at home after the game to eat pizza and watch a movie. My bickering children apparently didn't get the memo. This is exactly what my mom warned me about when I found out I would be having my kids close in age. She told me that there was bound to be plenty of arguing, but I sure wasn't expecting it to be this bad.

Of course, I also planned to have a husband in the house to help me break up the fighting. I guess nothing ended up like I expected after all.

Bryan ran to his house to check things out and then he will be back to join us for dinner. In the meantime, I'm attempting to take care of my evening chores, and we are working on baking individual pizzas.

Kate bursts into the laundry room, interrupting my train of thought. "Mom, I want to make a super mega pepperoni pizza and I'm not going to be able to if Kenzi hogs all of them! Tell her to stop."

I let out a heavy sigh. "Okay, I'm coming. Why can't you

girls just get along for three minutes so I can do the laundry?"

"Because Kenzi is mean." Kate replies. "And she doesn't know how to share."

Kate and I make our way to the kitchen, where I find Kate's pizza already covered in pepperoni and Kenzi sitting, holding the rest of the package in her hand. I motion for Kenzi to hand me the bag. Once she does, I divide the remaining slices, putting a pile in front of each child. "Okay, girls. You better finish up, so we can bake your pizzas."

Luckily, the ones I made for myself and Bryan are already done and ready to bake.

I turn and preheat the oven just as the doorbell rings loudly through the house. "That's probably Bryan. Okay, you two finish up and wait for me. No touching the oven while I'm gone." I instruct them before leaving the room. I make my way across the house and check the peephole at my front door. But instead of finding Bryan, there stands my late neighbor's daughter, Katheryn. My neighbor, Mrs. McBride, passed away just before Christmas. Katheryn moved out-of-town years ago, but still made a habit of coming to visit as often as possible. This is the first time I've seen her since the funeral.

"Katheryn. Hey. Come on in." I say, holding the screen door open for her.

Katheryn wearily steps inside. "Hey. I can't stay long. I just wanted to warn you we are having a garage sale tomorrow. So there will probably be people parking in front of your house and traipsing through your yard to buy my mom's random belongings." She groans.

I nod. "I totally understand. It will not bother me at all. I'm sorry again about your mom. I can imagine it's hard to go through and get rid of all her things."

She shakes her head. "It's been a lot." She agrees. "My mom was quite a... collector. I really regret not coming down more often and getting a head start on things."

I chuckle. "She would have never allowed that to happen. Her things were her treasures."

She groans. "I know, but now her treasures have become a giant pain for me. I thought about just donating it all, but Jack talked me out of it. And for good reasoning. I can't imagine how many trips I would have to take to the thrift store just to empty that place out. Her yard decor alone would be enough to fill the back of my Tahoe more than once. The thrift store is going to hate me if I can't scale it down some."

I lean out the door and look towards the neighbor's house. "Oh hey, speaking of yard decor. What are you doing with your mom's porch goose?"

For as long as I can remember, her mother had a concrete goose on her porch that she would dress in different outfits to correspond with the season. It's always been one of my favorite things about this neighborhood.

Katheryn lets out a heavy sigh. "That old chipped thing? I was honestly planning to just throw it in the trash. Why, do you want it?"

"Yes!" I reply a bit too quickly. "Please don't throw it away. I've always loved seeing how your mom styled her. I'd love to have her and bring her back to life."

She nods. "Okay, I'll dig out the tote full of clothes and have my husband carry her over later. She's pretty heavy." She says with a soft smile. "I bet Mom would be happy to know that she is going to have a new life."

"I've always loved that goose. My daycare kids always loved watching for her new outfits, too. It's been hard for them to

145

see her standing over there still wearing her Christmas dress in the middle of March. They'll be so excited to have her over here."

"Well, I'm glad to get that taken care of. Now, do you know anyone that likes old lady clothes? Weird knick knacks? Old books?"

I don't even try to hide the smile that spreads across my face. "Of course, I know just the people." I say with a laugh. "What time are you planning to open tomorrow? I'll alert the masses to get there first thing."

"Mom! The oven is beeping!" Kate yells from the kitchen, interrupting our conversation to let me know the oven is finally preheated.

"I'll be open by eight," Katheryn promises. "I'll let you get back to your girls."

"Thank you. We will see you in the morning." I say, before turning to answer Kate. "I'll be right there!"

"Okay, see you tomorrow and I'll have Jack bring that over tonight." She says, moving towards me and pulling me into a hug. As she steps back, she pauses. "Listen, thank you for loving my mom and letting her be a part of your life. I used to talk to her every Sunday evening, and she never failed to mention how you and the girls were doing. She loved watching your kids play in the yard and when they would bring her flowers in the spring. You were such a good neighbor to her, and you made her last few years on Earth even more beautiful. Thank you for loving on her."

I blink quickly, trying to fight back tears building in my eyes. "I'll never have a neighbor as great as she was. She always had banana bread or cookies for my girls. She never tired of listening to their stories or watching them dance around the yard. Not to mention the fact that she was always willing to mend and alter our clothes for us. We were blessed to have her, and she is irreplaceable. I can only hope my next neighbor will be half as good as she was."

"Okay, I have to go before you make me cry," Katheryn says, shaking her head. "I'll see you later, Madison."

"Bye. I'm sure we will be over tomorrow to do some shopping."

"Good. Tell everyone you can think of. I need this stuff to go to good homes." She says with a soft smile as she walks out the door and closes it gently behind her.

On my way back to the kitchen, I pull my phone from my pocket and text the group chat, inviting them to shop with me in the morning.

I put the pizzas in the oven just as a knock comes to the door once again. This time, I open the door to find Bryan on the other side.

"What's that look about?" He asks, raising a brow.

"I just got a goose. I'm very excited."

Bryan shakes his head. "I don't even want to ask."

* * *

At 7:45 am on the dot, a light knock sounds on my front door. I open it to find Tyler and Avery waiting on the other side. Avery is holding a cup of coffee and hands it to me.

"Bless you, woman." I say, taking the cup from her. "I hope you girls are ready to do some major shopping. Beatrice was quite a... collector."

"Oh, call it what it is, she was a hoarder." Tyler laughs. "But

147

that's okay, because I remember how much cool stuff she used to have. I'm hoping she has tons of books for me to add to the used section of my store. It seems like I can't keep cheap used books on the shelf for long."

"That's a good problem to have." I nod. "And I remember she was a bit of a reader. Maybe you'll get lucky."

"Hopefully, she read lots of smutty romance books. That seems to be a big seller in this town." Tyler laughs, nudging me. "Hey by the way, is that a goose on a porch?"

"Oh! I forgot!" I say, rushing onto the porch to admire my new decoration. I step onto the porch and admire my new friend. Next to the concrete goose sits a blue tote box. I lift the tote and carry it into the house. Quickly, I open the lid and squeal as I see the collection of goose clothes.

"Are those goose clothes?" Tyler asks with a chuckle. "You are so weird."

I grin. "Yes. Don't be jealous." I say as I scoop a small yellow raincoat and matching hat from the box and hold them up to show my friends. "This is going to be her very first outfit at her new home. I think I'll name her Reba Quackentire."

Avery laughs and shakes her head. "You are so weird. But, if it makes you happy, then I am just as excited about your porch goose as you are. Maybe you'll start a new trend around town."

"Oh, I'm not interested in being an Influencer," I say with a laugh. "I'll leave that up to you. But, I appreciate your support of my weird ideas. Honestly, I can't wait to show your brother this afternoon. He left around ten last night and I didn't think to check and see if the goose had been dropped off yet." I finish, just as Kenzi makes her way into the room. I turn to face my child. "Hey Kenzi, are you ready to go next door with us?"

Kenzi nods excitedly, causing the messy bun on top of her

head to fly around wildly. "I brought my purse." She says, holding up her hot pink cat shaped purse to show me. "And all my money is inside."

"Great! I bet you will find some sort of treasure over there." I say with a nod before calling for my other child. "Kate! Do you want to go next door with us?"

Kate walks into the room with a scowl. "Mom, I'm trying to watch my movie. Can I please stay here?"

I frown. Is this what it's like when your kids grow up? First, she wanted her own room, and now this? She doesn't even want to go next door with me and her sister?

I get it, of course. I'm proud of her for being so independent, but also, I yearn for the days when she was little and didn't want to leave my side. Where did that little girl disappear to?

"Yes, you can stay, but only because I will be right next door. Don't touch the stove or the microwave or, well, anything."

A grin spreads against Kate's face at the tiny victory. "I promise I won't do anything bad. I'm just going to lie in bed and watch TV."

"Okay." I nod. "I'll be right next door if you need me. Just open the door and yell for me."

Kate frowns. "I'm not a baby, you know."

"I know you're not." I insist. "It's just hard for me to see you growing up so much. I'll be back in just a little bit."

Kate offers me a small smile and then turns to make her way back to her room, closing her door behind her.

"She's growing up fast, mom," Avery mutters, as she puts an arm around my shoulders and pulls me into a side hug.

"Six going on sixteen." I reply. "I really thought I'd have another couple of years of her being a sweet little girl."

"It's just all a part of growing up, I think." Avery offers. "You are doing just fine. She wants to be independent, and that's normal. Besides, that means you've done a good job. You've taught her to be confident and comfortable on her own. That's a win."

"I hope you're right." I say.

"Besides, she's still sweet. She's just learning to be assertive. You'll appreciate that later."

"If I survive raising her first."

* * *

I'm supervising Kenzi as she thoroughly scours a bed sheet covered in Beatrice's beanie baby collection when Ava's royal blue SUV pulls to a stop at the curb in front of the house. I smile and offer her a wave as she exits the car and makes a beeline to Katheryn, who is sitting on the porch swing, nursing a mug of coffee.

"Hi." she says with a bright smile, throwing her long dark hair over her shoulder. "I'm Ava. I own Fawn Creek Homes and I'm friends with Madison." She says, cocking her head in my direction. "She told me you are planning to sell this beautiful place, and I just wanted to see if you have chosen a Realtor yet."

Katheryn smiles and stands to greet her. "Oh Ava, you are a godsend. I actually had it on my list to reach out to you today and see if you would be interested in representing us. Word around town is that you are the best girl for the job."

Ava beams. "Oh, thank you. I love helping people and yes, I'd love to help you, too." She pulls a card from her back pocket and hands it to Katheryn. "Here's my card if you don't already have one. Just shoot me a text and we will schedule a time to get started."

After finishing up with Katheryn, Ava makes her way down the old wooden stairs and towards the rest of our crew.

"Katheryn, how much do you want for these books?" Tyler asks, from her seat on the driveway surrounded by piles of novels that she's already found for herself.

"I'll take twenty dollars if you will take them all." Katheryn calls back.

Tyler looks around at the piles of books. "Are you sure? There are probably a hundred books here."

Katheryn nods, swallowing the sip of coffee she just took. "Please, you'd be doing me a favor. I'd almost pay you to take them for me."

Tyler shakes her head and moves across the lawn, pulling a twenty-dollar bill from her pocket and then makes her way back to load up the piles she had so diligently worked through.

"Do you have room in your store for those?" I ask with a laugh.

"I will eventually." She shrugs. "I never realized how much the people of Fawn Creek would appreciate a good used book store until I opened mine." She admits as she stands up and lifts a box to carry to her car.

"Told you so," Avery replies, in a sing-song voice. "But no, you didn't want to listen to me. Of course, the town is supporting you. It's exactly what downtown needed."

Ava bends down to pick up a box and follows Tyler to her car as Kenzi finally finishes deciding. "Okay mommy. I found a sea lion for me and a panda bear for Kate." She smiles widely. "I hope she likes it."

"I'm sure she will." I barely get the words out of my mouth before Kenzi is turning to make her way towards the porch.

"Did you find something?" Katheryn asks Kenzi.

Kenzi nods excitedly. "One for me and one for my sister." She announces proudly, showing the neighbor. "And I'm going to pay for them all by myself. How much money is it?"

Katheryn and I exchange a smile. "You know what? That is so nice of you to want to buy a gift for your sister. How about I just let you have these for free and you can keep your money? All you have to do is promise me you'll take very good care of them."

Kenzi's eyes widen. "Really?!" she squeals. "Mom, did you hear that?"

I nod. "I did. That was very nice, and you need to make sure you say thank you."

"Thank you!" Kenzi shouts, smiling up at the neighbor. "I will take such good care of them and I'll make Kate promise to love hers, too."

"Perfect." Katheryn grins. "Then we are even." She assures Kenzi as I make my way over to them. My arms are full of a floral quilt, several pink curtains in assorted sizes, and some lace tablecloths. I add my findings to the pile I had already started that contains Beatrice's entire set of kitchen decor from the nineties.

Katheryn laughs as she picks up a cookie jar of a goose wearing a bonnet, "You're really leaning in to this goose thing, huh?" She says with a laugh.

"I am slowly working on redecorating my house. I want to give it some character and what better way to do that than with a few fun whimsical touches?"

"I love it." Katheryn says with a smile. "You've always been so fun. It just makes sense that you'd grow up to teach daycare. I bet those kids have a blast with you."

"They do!" Avery chimes in, her arms full of clothes from Beatrice's collection. "Katheryn, what are you going to do with all this leftover stuff?"

Katheryn shakes her head. "I don't know. I guess it'll have to go to the thrift store."

Ava chimes in. "Hey, Madison, maybe you could take what's left over and we can have a yard sale of our own. To raise money for the storm shelter. Seriously. I'll donate stuff to it and then come shop everyone else's crap."

"What storm shelter?" Katheryn asks.

"Oh, I run a daycare out of my house and I am tired of putting kids in the car and racing to the church, so I applied for a grant to get a shelter. Who knows if I'll even get it, but if I do, it'll only part for part of it. I'll have to come up with a couple thousand dollars to pay for my portion."

"Oh, that's a good idea." Katheryn nods. "I'd happily give you what's left here so you can use it for your sale."

I pause and look around at all the women staring at me. "So, I guess we're doing this, then?"

"Yes." Avery smiles. "And we will help you. I love a good yard sale and if it makes it easier for you to take care of my kid for years to come, then I'm in." She promises, carrying an armload of clothing over to Katheryn.

Katheryn examines the pile with wide eyes.

"I'm opening a mobile boutique." Avery explains away the pile. "My husband bought me an old camper and I want to make sure I have both new and used clothing to offer when I finally do events."

"That's amazing." Katheryn says, as she folds each item and places them in a plastic grocery bag. "That makes me want to clean out my closet."

"Well, donate it to her sale and I will snatch it all up." Avery says with a laugh.

Ava shakes her head. "We are going to have your storm shelter in no time."

Chapter 19

"Here, Freckles." Bryan says with a grin, as he places a opened can of Diet Dr. Pepper on the porch next to me and goes back to his spot in the yard.

"Thank you," I say, picking up the can and stepping back on to the porch to examine my handiwork. "How'd you know I hate opening my own cans?"

Bryan grins. "I didn't. I just like doing things for you, I guess. It makes me feel good."

"I like it too. Are you sure the pink isn't too much?" I ask, eyeing the front door that I just finished painting. I was feeling a lot more confident when I decided to use my leftover baby pink paint on my front door than I am now.

"Do you like it?" Bryan asks, turning the question around on me.

"Yes." I nod.

"Then who cares if someone else thinks it's too much? I think it's perfect. It's fun and playful, just like you are. And your goose looks pretty good next to it, too."

I glance over at the shutters Bryan is building to hang on the exterior of the house next to the windows. They are the same shade of light pink I used for the door. "Those shutters are going to pop against the white siding on the house. Thank you so much for helping me with all this. I've wanted to give the front of the house some updates for a while now, but I had been afraid to do it. You sure get stuck with a lot of work while you're home."

Bryan shrugs. "It's no problem. Besides, once we finally get done decorating your place, you can come over and help me decorate mine."

I scoff. "Your bachelor pad? You really want to let me help with that? That's your space."

Bryan smiles softly. "Maybe I want it to feel like OUR space." He says with a slight blush of his cheeks, just as a beeping sound comes from inside the house.

"Ah, the brownies are done!" I laugh, looking down at my paint covered hands.

"I'll get them. You just stay here and finish that door." He says with a laugh as he makes his way back into the house.

Ben had called this afternoon to ask if the girls could go with him to his mom's house for her birthday dinner. While I wanted to say no, because it is my weekend after all, I also didn't want them to miss out on the fun. Otherwise, they would have just been bored hanging out at home.

After the girls left, we worked on a few projects around the house and decided to celebrate with a tray of brownies and some vanilla ice cream. Turns out, not only is Bryan great at fixing cars and building shutters, but he also has his favorite homemade brownie recipe memorized. The brownies are done just in time to share with the girls when they get back.

Speaking of the devil, there's Ben now. He pulls his truck to a stop at the curb and quickly the girls climb out of the backseat and make their way towards me.

"Mommy! I love the door! It's pink, my favorite color!"

Kenzi squeals.

"Mine too." I say with a smile. "Don't touch it on your way by. It's still wet. Go on in and I'll be in there in a second." I tell the girls as they make their way inside. I sit my paintbrush down in my tray and turn to find Ben staring with a disgusted look on his face.

"You painted the door pink? Why?"

I shrug. "Why not? It makes me happy, and it's just paint."

"All this painting you're doing is just you throwing money away. If you ever want to sell this house, you'll have to repaint it all. Or what if a guy wants to move in with you? He will not want to live in a girly house."

I shake my head. "Honestly, I'm not worried about it right now. I lived in this white on white house for years because of resale value. Maybe I don't want to sell it. Maybe I'll keep it forever. It's really none of your concern."

Ben shakes his head. "You're right, Madison. You keep on destroying your property value and living your delusional life, but one day you're going to regret this. Sorry I tried to help."

I furrow my brows. "Goodbye Ben." I say, turning and walking into the house, leaving the argument and my new pink door behind me.

He's the last person I'm going to let ruin my good night. I make my way into the kitchen and pause in the doorway as I see Bryan, Kenzi, and Kate at the counter with their brownies and ice cream. Kate and Kenzi are sitting on bar stools and Bryan is leaning against the counter. When I enter the room, they all turn to look at me. My anger towards Ben instantly melts away. These are my people. The loves of my life and my biggest supporters.

"There you are," Bryan says with a smile, as he moves to add some ice cream to my bowl. He smiles and slides it towards the space next to him. "Come join us."

Kate looks up from her bowl. "Were you and dad arguing?"

I shake my head, staring down into my bowl. "No, he just didn't like my door color. Don't worry about it."

"Dad's a jerk, anyway." Kate mutters, looking down at her own bowl.

I frown. "Kate, that's not very nice."

"She's just mad at him because he won't let us get a trampoline." Kenzi informs me.

Kate rolls her eyes. "He told us if we want one, we have to get one at your house. I told him you can't have one because of the daycare kids."

I nod. It's true, and Ben knows that, too. Kate has wanted a trampoline for a couple of years now after playing on one at a friend's house. But, since I watch kids in our house, I can't have one, according to the state. It's too much of a liability.

"I'm sorry girls. You know I'd let you have one in a heartbeat if I could. I loved jumping on a trampoline when I was a kid."

"Daddy said they are too dangerous and he can't pay our hospital bills." Kenzi adds.

I frown. "I'm sorry girls."

Kate shrugs. "It's fine. I just thought maybe he'd let us since you couldn't. I'll just have to find a friend with a trampoline so I can go to their house and play."

* * *

After putting the girls to bed, Bryan and I sit out on my porch swing, wrapped in a blanket.

"I'm happy you came home this weekend. I figured you wouldn't be back for a while."

"Well, it's going to be at least another two weeks before I can make it back again. I wish I could swing it every weekend. We are trying to finish up a lot of stuff in the shop at work."

"That's okay." I assure him. "Except it makes me feel bad that I put you to work this weekend." I admit.

"Nonsense. It felt good to help you with your projects. And hang out with the girls. They are great kids."

I nod. "They really are. And they like you a lot. Believe me, you'd know it if they didn't like you."

"I like them, too." He admits, squeezing me tight with his arm around me. "Their mom isn't so bad either."

I smirk. "Yeah, I think she has a thing for you, too."

"I mean. I think I may be in love with their mom," Bryan admits, turning to raise a brow at me. "Of course, I wouldn't want her to say that back to me if she wasn't ready. I just think that she should know."

I pause and look up at the dark night sky before turning back to him. "That's the thing. I think she loves you, too. Even if it seems soon." I admit, leaning up to meet his lips with mine.

"Maybe it's not soon. Maybe I've just been waiting for you for a long, long time." He decides as our lips collide.

* * *

"Morning!" Becca calls out as I open the door and welcome her into the house.

Today is the first day of Spring Break and the first day of her working as my helper.

"I didn't know what to wear or what to bring or…" Becca trails off. "I'm a little nervous."

"Don't be." I shake my head and eye her outfit. She's wearing a T-shirt and leggings with sneakers. "They are just kids. And you look great. You just need to wear clothes that will allow you to move and play and not be sad if you stain them. You don't need to bring anything. I'll even feed you. Just don't stress and have fun."

"That makes me feel a lot better." Becca admits. "I'm really excited to help."

"Well, only a few kids are here so far. It's just a few of our regulars for now. Kate, Kenzi, Piper, Juliet and Carson." I say, pointing out each kid. "Here, in a bit, my other two regulars, Anna and David, will be here. Then, we were also able to take on three school aged kids. Their names are Joey, Lexi and Zane."

Becca already looks overwhelmed. "Hey." I say, turning to face her. "It'll be okay. Follow my lead. We've got this."

"Okay, we've got this." She repeats.

* * *

We are standing in the yard while the kids play when I check the time. "Hey guys! It's time to get inside for lunch!" I call out to them.

Becca turns to her group that is playing a game of Simon Says. "Simon Says, walk to Miss Madi!" She calls out to them. "Man. Just in time, too. I'm exhausted." She admits when she reaches me.

"They definitely know how to wear you out." I agree, as I line the kids up to head inside. I pause and do a quick headcount to make sure we have them all.

"Always count heads everywhere you go." I inform her. "You never know when a kid will decide to run off for an adventure or take a nap when you're inside."

"Got it." She nods. "This really has been a fun day."

"It's a fun job, mostly. What age group do you want to teach?"

Becca shrugs as we make our way into the house. "I'm not sure. I thought about upper elementary, but now I think I like the younger kids. They're so sweet."

"Friends, time to line up to wash your hands, then have a seat on the rug in the living room while I get food ready." I command. "They really are!" I agree with Becca. "They know how to make you feel loved when you need it the most. Well, I hope you enjoy this week because if so I'd love to have an assistant this summer. There's always a need for childcare over the summer and it would bless a lot of people if we could offer it."

"Count me in."

Chapter 20

"Okay, Becca, if you just want to finish loading the dishwasher, I'll go get the mail and you can head home." I call out as I follow Carson and Eric on their way out the door.

It's Friday and my assistant has officially survived Spring Break.

"Dad, look at the goose today!" Carson giggles. "She's wearing a dress."

"That's a pretty silly goose." Eric says with a laugh before turning back to look at me. "How many outfits do you have for that thing?"

"A lot." I admit. "But I want you to know that I inherited them all from the neighbor."

Eric lifts his eyes towards the house next door and raises a brow. "That neighbor?"

I follow his gaze to see who he's looking at, and find Ava standing on the porch of the house next door. "Uh, no. Actually, that's Ava. Piper's mom."

"Oh, I remember her well." He says, blushing.

I laugh and shake my head. I had a feeling when they met that the crush was mutual. "She's a Realtor and probably over there to do a showing."

"Interesting." He nods, helping Carson into the car. "Well,

I'll see you on Monday. Have a good weekend."

"See you Monday. You too!" I say before walking to the street to retrieve my mail, and call out to Ava. "Finally getting that place listed?" I ask.

Ava shakes her head and begins her descent down the wooden porch. "No, even better, actually." She says with a grin, watching me pull my mail from the mailbox.

"What could be better than that?" I ask.

"What would you think about having a neighbor that you're already friends with?"

I furrow my brows. "Who? You know I don't have that many people I actually consider to be my friends, right? Just you, Avery, Tyler and Sierra." I say, pulling a single letter from my mailbox.

"Well, it's one of those." She teases.

My eyes widen. "Wait. It's you? Are you buying this place?"

"Yes! I just signed a contract with Katheryn. I'll be closing in thirty days. "

I pull Ava into a hug. "This is amazing! I had no idea you were even interested in buying!"

"I wasn't." She admits. "Until I started walking around inside the house. It's gorgeous and so full of character. I couldn't pass it up. Besides, living next to you guys? Icing on the cake."

"I'm so happy for you. And for me. It will be great to have you as a neighbor. Kate is going to lose her mind." I tell her, stepping back to put my hands on my hips. Then, I remember the letter in my hand. I examine the return address. "Hey, I think this is about the grant." I say, wasting no time to open the envelope.

Ava pauses and waits while I read over the letter. I put my

hand over my mouth to keep myself from screaming. "Ava. We did it! I got the grant! It's been approved. I just have to get it scheduled and they will pay their portion to the installer." I report, reading back over the letter. "Shit, I'm going to have to come up with twenty-five hundred dollars to cover my portion."

Ava shakes her head. "We will figure it out in plenty of time before your install appointment. Call and get on the books. Who knows how long it'll take to even get them out here? You leave the rest to me and Avery. We will get it figured out."

I bite the inside of my lip. "Okay, if you say so. I guess it's time to organize my garage full of yard sale stuff, isn't it?"

* * *

"Are you sure you want to help me with this?" I ask, eyeballing Bryan as he drops the tailgate on his truck and begins pulling out boxes.

He raises a brow and looks at me like I've lost my mind. "Yes, woman, of course I do."

I frown. "I just can't imagine this is how you want to spend your weekend at home. You haven't been home in two weeks and now you're here. Stuck, sitting in my yard helping me sell old clothes for a dollar a piece."

Bryan places the boxes he's holding down in the driveway and then moves towards me, pulling me close to him. "First off. I want to help you raise the money for this storm shelter as soon as possible. I would spend every weekend hanging out in your yard helping you sell shit for a dollar if that means that I can rest easy knowing that you and the girls are safe during storm season." He confesses kissing the top of my head. "Second, I'm not just going to be sitting around. I am going to be mowing the backyard, fixing the fence, checking the oil in your van, and every other thing I can find around here that needs done."

I shake my head and pull away to eye him suspiciously. "No, that's unnecessary. You are here to relax at home for a long weekend, not to play Mr. Handyman around my house."

"I wanna do both." He says, leaning down to kiss me. "I just want to be where you are. And it's okay that where you are is in your front yard selling tables full of random crap." He laughs. "What can we do to get started?"

I pause and look around. "Well, I thought I'd wait for your sister to get here since she's a yard sale addict, but last I knew, she was still at work. So, I guess let's start by setting up the tables." I say, motioning towards the pile of folding tables leaning against the garage.

"Where did you get all of those?" Bryan laughs.

"They belong to the church. The youth pastor even dropped them off for me. Once I told them what I was raising money for, they were so happy to lend them over."

"Man, your daycare kids must be a real pain in the ass when you take them to the storm shelter in the church basement." Bryan teases. "Hell, the church might just give you the full amount of money you need for your shelter, if that's the case."

"My kids are angels." I inform him, lightly swatting at his arm. "But, that truly would open up some space in there during weekdays if I didn't have a bunch of kids with me."

"Well, that's the goal for the weekend, then." Bryan says, getting back to work on setting up tables. "Hopefully by this time tomorrow night you'll at least have a good chunk of cash to go towards your goal."

"I hope so. My appointment is still a month out, but I want to have cash in hand long before then." I say as I watch Avery pull up to the curb in front of the house. "Thank goodness, the yard sale queen has arrived."

Bryan watches as Avery opens the back of her SUV and turns to look at us. "I think we're going to need more tables."

* * *

"Wow." My mom's voice cuts through the crowd in my yard as she crosses my driveway with Kenzi and Kate in tow. "You guys really pulled this together."

I lean down to tell both of the girls hi and give them a hug before standing to greet my mom. The girls race into the house.

"We really did. Thank you so much for keeping the girls last night so I could get all of this ready."

She waves me off. "We love having them at the house. They are so fun. I would have kept them longer, but they were pretty excited to get back here and start on their lemonade stand."

I nod. "Oh yes. They have been talking about it all week. Pink lemonade and store-bought cookies for the win." I say with a laugh. "They are determined that they are going to single-handedly reach the goal on their own."

"Speaking of," Mom pauses, reaching into her pocket. "Dad and I want to help your cause." She says, handing me a folded slip of paper.

I open the paper and find that it's a check for five hundred dollars. I shake my head. "Mom, you don't have to do this. You and dad have already done so much for me. And you help so

166

much with the girls...." I attempt to hand the check back.

"And we want to help with this, too." She insists, pushing my hand back. "This is for a good cause, and you can't put a price on keeping my grand babies safe." She folds her arms in front of her chest. "I'm not taking no for an answer, so just take the check."

I nod, reading the paper once more before folding it and putting it in my pocket. "Thank you." I say, leaning in to give her a hug. The sound of the screen door opening breaks us apart. I turn to find the girls and Bryan waiting on the porch for me.

"Hey Madi, are you ready for the girls to set up their lemon-ade stand? They are begging me to bring things out for them." He says with a chuckle.

I smile brightly. "Yes! We should definitely get that started. They have a lot of money they plan to make today."

"Mom, thanks again for your help and for the check." I say, giving her another hug.

"You're welcome. Good luck today." She says, waving as she makes her way to the street. "Let me know how it goes!"

* * *

"Mom, we are going to need more lemonade soon." Kate says, turning to face me while I'm tallying a total from a woman with a box full of old clothes.

"Um, yes. Give me just a second, Kate, and I'll go grab you some. I just need to finish up here." I say, trying not to lose my count.

"I'll get it," Bryan says, jumping up to make his way inside.

It's noon. Avery just left to pick up lunch. The girls are almost done with their second pitcher of lemonade and of course this is when the biggest rush we've had all day hits.

"Thank you." I say to Bryan before turning my attention back to the woman. "That'll be twenty-two dollars."

"Will you take twenty?" She counters.

"Yes, that's fine." I nod, not willing to argue over a couple of dollars considering the amount of stuff she is getting off my lawn for me.

"Well, aren't you a sight for sore eyes?" A man's voice causes me to start.

I turn my head in the direction that it came from and find the source. But it's no one I recognize. Apparently, that is clear in my expression.

"You don't remember me, do you?" He teases.

I shake my head. "No, I'm sorry. I don't."

"It's okay." He says, crossing the lawn towards me before he leans on the porch railing. "It's me. Seth Rhodes."

I pause, trying to think of who he is, but still nothing clicks.

"We went to junior high together." He adds. "I moved out of town at the end of seventh grade. We actually shared a pretty epic kiss in Cory Anderson's basement the summer before seventh grade started while playing spin the bottle. I had the biggest crush on you and you had just started dating that douche bag, Ben Porter. Whatever happened to him, anyway?"

I laugh. "Well, I married him."

Seth's face immediately turns a bright shade of pink. "Shit. Sorry. I've never been great at not sticking my foot in my mouth." He admits.

I lower my voice. "Well, if it's any consolation prize, I did later divorce him, so I will not disagree with you labeling him as a douche bag. But maybe try not to call him that again in front of his kids." I say, pointing to my daughters who are sitting in lawn chairs playing a game on their tablets between customers. "Luckily for me, I think they are too busy playing their game to have heard you."

He turns to look at the kids and then back at me. "My bad, I didn't see them there." He admits, leaning in closer. "So, does that mean that you're available? I don't know about you, but I've learned a lot of things since that spin the bottle kiss. I'm only in town for the weekend, but...."

I shake my head. "No, I...." I say, but Bryan makes his way out the front door carrying a pitcher of pink lemonade and interrupts the moment. Thank goodness.

Seth nods to acknowledge him and watches as he makes his way towards the girls. "I see. Too late, again." Seth laughs. "Well, it was nice seeing you, but I guess I'll get out of your hair." He quickly spits out before turning on his heel and making his way back towards a Toyota Camry parked at the curb.

Bryan watches as Seth speed walks past and then turns to join me back on the porch. "What was that about?"

"You saved my life." I say with a chuckle. "Try not to be jealous, but I guess I kissed that guy in seventh grade. I honestly don't remember it, but he did."

Bryan shakes his head. "And he said something about it?"

"He told me he's learned a thing or two since then." I report, trying to stifle a laugh.

Bryan groans. "Well, I should have known that if I'm going to date a small town hottie, I'm probably going to run into her ex lovers from time to time." He teases. "And shit. I hope he's learned a few things since junior high."

"I think he was about to show me before you walked out and saved the day. Please never leave me out here alone again."

"I'll try," Bryan says with a wink.

I look up just in time to see an old silver Volkswagen Beetle park on the curb in front of the house. "Oh slug bug!" I shout and lightly punch Bryan's arm. "Now a man with one of those might steal me away, though." I admit with a wink as an older gentleman exits the car and makes this way towards the yard sale goodies.

"A VW bug? Really?" Bryan asks with a laugh.

"Absolutely. That's my dream car." I confirm. "My grandpa had one when I was a kid and I loved it. It was an old rattly thing, and it was my favorite car in the world. It had no carpet or headliner. The exterior was primer grey, the radio didn't work, it had no heat or A/C and I couldn't hear a word he said to me while I was in the backseat of that noisy old thing, but I didn't care. I would have ridden in the car with him to the end of the Earth if he let me. The day he sold it, you would have thought that I lost my best friend. Honestly, I was devastated. I guess my delusional self thought I was going to inherit it one day, but I was only eleven and he needed the money." I shake my head and watch the old man pillage through the tables of odds and ends. "Every time I see one of those cars, I think of him. I miss him so much but those cars remind me of those days. He's been gone a long time, but seeing one makes me feel close to him again."

"Mom! We're getting bored." Kate says, as she makes her way towards me from his lemonade table. "When can we go inside?"

I glance toward the girls' stand. The new pitcher of lemonade Bryan made is still sitting untouched on the table and both girls look as though they could use a nap. Just then, Avery pulls up with take out Mexican food to save the day.

"Perfect timing!" I announce. "Lunch has arrived! Girls, I'll bring your stuff inside so it doesn't get too hot in the sun while you eat and play for a bit." I pick up the jar of money from the table and count the dollar bills inside. I've been collecting their money every so often and keeping a tally of what they raised. "Girls, you made over $100 today. You did a good job!"

"Good. I need a taco." Kenzi groans. "Lemonade selling is hard work."

Yep, that kid is definitely mine.

* * *

"Well, how'd we do?" Bryan asks, entering the kitchen to find me standing at the dining table. I just finished counting the money from the sale.

"$973 total." I reply. "So close to a thousand. Not bad for a day's work, though."

"After the amount of clothes you and Avery bought for yourselves, I'm shocked we had anything left at all." Bryan laughs.

"Hey." I scoff. "We paid for it all fair and square. I have been telling Avery I wanted to go thrifting for a new wardrobe, so this was killing two birds with one stone. You won't complain when you see me in what I got."

"I can't wait." He says with a wink as he pulls his wallet from his pocket. He pulls out two bills, a twenty and a ten before handing them over to me. "Here, now you have over a thousand. And don't even say you're not going to take it. Just do it. I want to help."

I roll my eyes and take the cash, adding it to my pile. "Well, between this and the check my mom brought, we are at fifteen hundred. Only a thousand more to go, but I only have a month to pull it off." I let out a groan.

"Oh, I bet it won't take that long," Bryan says, waving me off.

"I'm sure you'll have it figured out in no time."

Chapter 21

"Okay." Avery says, stepping back to assess the table in front of her. She's been working diligently for the last half hour to organize all the snacks for tonight's event. All along the eight-foot table, she's lined it with a stack of pizza boxes plus colorful bowls full of chips, Chex Mix, goldfish crackers, and packages of fruit snacks. On either side, she has a fruit tray and then next to the table there's a station filled with drink options; water bottles, juice and tea. "Do you think I went too far?"

I shake my head quickly. "No way, that looks great. The kids are going to love it and so will their parents."

"Okay good. What else can I do to help you?" She asks, moving to take a seat next to me at the sign-in table.

I look over the list on my phone and shake my head. "We are all ready to go. We just have to wait for our volunteers to get here and then open the doors for the kids at five-thirty."

"I have to hand it to you, Madi. When you proposed the idea of hosting a parents' night out for a fundraiser, I never thought it would have exploded like this. It was a great idea."

"The parents of Fawn Creek thought so too." I say with a laugh. "I still can't believe we sold out of tickets in two weeks. At twenty-five bucks a kid for thirty kids, we raised another seven hundred and fifty bucks."

When I brought up the idea of doing this event for a fundraiser, I wasn't sure if it would really bring in much money. However, the parents of Fawn Creek were more than ready to get out for a date night now that the weather is better. In fact, the response was so overwhelming we had to move the event from my house to the church gymnasium. Now, instead of it being just me and a helper, we have a list of volunteers that are ready with snacks, games, movies and goody bags for thirty kids to come hang out while their parents get a much-needed date night.

"Of course they sold out that fast." Avery laughs. "Everyone in this town knows that you are the elite daycare provider around here. From the lesson plans you do and share with the parents so we know what our kids are learning about each week, to the outdoor play activities and the sensory experiences. Don't even get me started on the nutritious meals and the field trips you organize. Every parent in this town wishes their kid could come to your daycare. Everyone here wants you to open your own center so you can take on more kids. Except, of course, those of us that already are lucky enough to have you. We don't want to share."

"That's really nice of you to say those things." I say, reaching an arm out to hug my friend.

"I only say it because it's true. You are a blessing to these kids and all of their parents. We love you and we are thankful for you and we want to help you succeed. If this will help make your days easier when taking care of our kids, then we are all in." She says with a smile, hugging me back.

Just then, I hear the door to the gym click open. Assuming it's an early arrival, I turn to tell them we don't open for another half hour, but instead Bryan walks through the door.

"Bryan!" I shout, standing from the table to move towards him. "What are you doing here? You didn't tell me you were coming to town." I say, standing on tiptoe to quickly kiss his lips.

"I know, dummy, that's what a surprise is." He answers with a chuckle before wrapping his arms around my body and lifting me from the ground to kiss me once more. "I just missed you and thought maybe you could use one more helper tonight."

I nod. "I would love that. You know we will be here until midnight, right?" I ask, raising a brow.

"Yeah, that's fine." He says, waving me off. "I had an energy drink on my way here and I'm ready to.. well, do whatever you tell me to."

"Bryan's baby bootcamp!" Avery exclaims.

He furrows his brows. "Say what, now?"

"You can have the kids do PT to burn off some energy after they get done snacking." Avery laughs. "Push up and sit up contest. Jumping jacks, you know, the works. Get them all nice and worn out before they lay down to watch a movie."

Bryan laughs. "You know what? I actually don't hate that idea at all. I'm in."

"Good." I say, checking my watch. "Well, get ready because our first kids will arrive in the next ten minutes."

"Bring it on."

* * *

"I have never been more exhausted in my life." Nathan says, as he leans against the gym wall and slides down to sit next to me. "How do you do this every day?" He groans.

"Well, usually I don't have thirty kids to take care of at one time... and they go home long before midnight." I say with a yawn before turning to look at my group of volunteers. "Guys, I can't thank you enough for forfeiting your Saturday night to help me. I know there are a million things you'd rather be doing."

"It was actually a lot of fun." Becca pipes up. "Thanks for asking us."

"Thank mom for volunteering us," Nathan groans. "I'm going to be sore for days after playing gaga ball with those kids. I'm pretty sure a few of them were out for blood."

I laugh. "You'll be just fine, tough guy. Why don't you guys take the rest of the pizza with you and head on home? We have just about everything cleaned up here." I say, looking around the space. Luckily, we had enough helpers that we could stay on top of things, mostly.

"Are you sure?" Becca asks. "We don't mind staying to help."

Nathan darts his eyes to hers and lifts a brow as though to start a silent argument.

"Very sure. Go." I say, waving them off. "Thank you both so much."

"We are going to head out, too." Ava says, entering the room to gather Piper. "The kitchen is all cleaned up and closed down, and the trash is out."

"Bless you, woman." I say with a grin as I watch Avery and Bryan finish putting away the last of the play equipment, and mom putting away the push broom. "I think we aren't too far behind you, either."

Mom makes her way over to us. "Girls, what do you think

about having a sleepover at Grammy' tonight?"

"Really?" Kenzi squeals.

"Really." she confirms before turning to me. "I figure I'll give you some... quiet time for the rest of the evening." She adds, nudging her head towards Bryan.

"Thank you." I whisper.

"Girls, let's go," Mom says, motioning to the door.

"We don't even have to go home and change clothes because we're already in our pjs!" Kenzi reports excitedly. "Bye Mommy!"

"Bye mom!" Kate echoes with a smile and a wave as they make their way out the door.

"Well. What do you think? Your place or mine?" Bryan asks with a wink as he and Avery make their way towards us.

"Gross." Avery scrunches her face.

"If you think that's gross, you should hear what I'm going to do with her when we get to her house."

"Goodnight." Avery holds up her hands in an effort to make him stop talking. "Thanks for coming to help. I'm going to go wash my brain out with soap now."

"I love getting on her nerves." He says with a laugh, as he leads me towards the door.

"You're pretty dang good at it, too."

* * *

"Okay, I'm going to get out of here so we don't have to answer a million questions when the girls get home," Bryan says with a laugh. "After you all get up and around, call me and I'll come get you. I have a surprise for the girls."

"What did you get them?" I ask, following him to the front door.

"You'll find out," He teases, kissing me once more. "I love you."

"I love you, too. We will be there in a couple of hours, I'm sure." I assure him, as I pause in the doorway. I watch as he steps off the porch and walks across the yard to his truck before turning to look at Ava's house. She's sitting on the porch with her cup of coffee.

"Hey! Just the person I was waiting to see." Ava jumps up from her seat and runs across my yard with a stack of papers in her hand.

I hold the door open for her. "What? Were you sitting over there stalking me?"

"Kinda. I was just so excited to show you how we're going to raise the last of your storm shelter money, but I didn't want to interrupt anything with you and Bryan." Ava hands me the stack of tickets printed on cardstock she carried over with her.

"A half a hog?" I ask, reading over the ticket.

"Yes."

"What.. what does that even mean?" I ask, shaking my head. "All I can picture is a half of an actual pig sticking out of a cooler."

"You were definitely not a 4-H kid, were you?" Ava laughs. "A half a hog is a big deal! One hog is so much meat. Bacon, pork chops, sausage…. It's like seventy to ninety pounds of meat. And it's good meat at that. My uncle donated the pig and the processing. People are going to love this. Let's sell tickets for $10 a piece. We only need to sell a minimum of seventy-five. Then, we will draw for a winner in two weeks on Facebook live."

I nod. "Okay. That sounds great, actually. Thank you and thank your uncle for me, too."

"I will," Ava beams, handing me a stack of tickets. "But for now, let's get to work. I'll post all over social media as soon as I get home. Give a few to each daycare, kid, too."

I nod. "We should take some to the coffee shop, the bookstore and Myrtles, too."

"And the flower shop, too! I'll do that tomorrow after I drop off Ava. We will have the last of your money raised in no time."

"That's good because my install appointment is coming up quickly and I refuse to ask anyone for help."

"I know. You're stubborn as hell, but I love you, so it's okay. We've got this all under control. You take care of our kids. Let us take care of you."

* * *

"Okay girls, cover your eyes and don't look until I say you can," Bryan instructs my daughters in the backseat of his truck. "And I mean it."

While trying to stifle their giggles, both girls do as they are told. The anticipation of Bryan pulling into his long driveway is obviously killing them.

Bryan puts the truck in park and turns back to look at the kids. "Okay, girls. Uncover your eyes and look into the backyard." He says.

Kate and Kenzi do as they are told, straining their necks and then stretching tall to look past the house.

"Wait. What is that?" Kate asks, turning her head to the side as though it will give her a better view.

"It's a big, black circle." Kenzi decides.

Bryan laughs. "I think you guys need to get out of the truck and go inspect it a bit closer."

I raise a brow to Bryan and open my door, climbing out to help Kenzi get out of her car seat. Bryan climbs out to help Kate with her own. Together, the girls run towards the big circle in the yard.

I turn to Bryan, making sure my voice is low. "What is it?"

He grins. "An in ground trampoline."

I shake my head and laugh. "Are you kidding me? What are you going to do with that?"

Bryan squeezes my hand. "Well, it's not for me, Freckles. It's for the girls."

I watch as the girls approach their surprise and both shriek. "Mom! It's a trampoline. It's like our own trampoline park at Bryan's house!"

Kenzi runs back towards us and wraps her arms around Bryan, hugging him tightly. "Thank you! I love it. Can we play on it?"

"Yes, of course." He nods. "Take your shoes off and knock yourselves out."

"But not literally." I add. "Be careful!"

"We will!" They reply in unison as they work to slip off their shoes and climb onto the black canvas.

Bryan laces his hand in mine as we finish our walk towards them. He looks around. "We are going to need a hammock or something out here. And maybe a hot tub."

I laugh. "Well, I'm glad you're starting small. I can't believe you got them a trampoline." I say, shaking my head.

"Well, I remember hearing how sad Kate was about not being able to have one at your house. So, I figured why not have one here? Maybe they will want to spend more time here if they have some things of their own."

I raise a brow. "Are you bribing my children?"

He shrugs. "Maybe a little. I might be bribing you, too. If they have something to keep them entertained, then maybe you'll want to be out here more, too."

I blush. "Bryan, we love spending time with you. I just don't want to intrude on your solitude. You were the one that told me you don't love being surrounded by people, and I don't want to overstep that boundary."

Bryan turns towards me and wraps his arm around my waist, pulling me close to his chest. "Freckles, you and the girls are the only people I want to be around as much as I can. I want you here. All the time. Every chance I get," He confesses, as I look up at him and stand on tiptoe to kiss his lips. "I love you."

"I love you, too." I say back, before crashing my lips back into his.

Bryan grins wide and then pulls me tight against his chest. I rest my head there, overlooking the open acreage behind his house. I narrow my eyes as they land on an enormous pile of dirt.

"Is that dirt pile from you digging the hole for the trampoline?" I ask, nudging my head towards it.

"Yes, but don't get it twisted. Cody came over with the backhoe and dug it for me. I would have died doing it by myself."

"What are you going to do with it?"

He pauses and looks back at it. "Well, I figured it would just sit there for now. What do you need a pile of dirt for?"

I grin. "Oh, I have an idea. I'm just going to need you to hang on to it until next month."

"I promise it's not going anywhere."

Chapter 22

"Good morning! It's a busy day." Avery says, walking into the house with Juliet perched on her hip. I'm not sure if she is talking about the fact that the installers for the storm shelter are coming today, or that today is the day that her brother will officially move back to Fawn Creek. Either way, she's right.

Last week, just in the nick of time, we finished selling tickets for our storm shelter fundraiser. We ended up selling one hundred tickets, instead of the seventy-five that we needed. This allowed us to not only fund what we need for the shelter, but to buy some extras as well. We are now the owners of a potty chair to put inside the shelter, because who knows when an emergency will arise, especially when you are potty training toddlers. I also had enough leftover money to order a little library for the front yard.

"You're telling me." I say, plopping down on a bar stool in the kitchen.

She frowns. "You don't seem excited. Is everything okay? Did my brother do something wrong? Because I'm telling you, I will handle him if I need to."

I shake my head. "No. I'm just overwhelmed. There is a lot going on today. And I hate to admit it but, your brother moving to town means that it's real. It's a little scary. Dating from a distance was one thing, but now we are going to have access to each other every day."

Avery moves towards me and rests her hands on my shoulders. "Of course it's real. This is what you two have been waiting for. This is what will make the last two months of living separately all worth it."

I chew on my lip and pause for a second. "True. But what if he moves here and realizes he doesn't actually like me that much? What if he figures out that taking on a divorced woman with a bunch of baggage and two kids is too much?"

Avery shakes her head. "My brother knows exactly what he's getting into. He loves you. He loves the girls. It pains me to admit it after years of thinking that he's nothing but an asshole, but honestly, he is total stepdad material. He will not regret any of this. I'm sure of it."

"And what if I hate him? What if we spent all this time leading up to this and I figure out that I can't stand him?"

"Then I won't blame you." She teases. "I'm kidding. Madison, that will not happen. Some people are just meant to be together. They become a couple and suddenly they just jive so well. One is high where the other is low. That's you guys. You're extroverted, he's introverted. You're pink and cheery. He's more oil stained. Opposites attract. I truly believe he is your missing piece. You are meant to be together and I'm so excited to see you guys finally be in the same place."

"Me too." I nod. "I'm just nervous, I guess. It's been a weird year for me and trusting someone with my heart again feels so heavy." I admit.

"Don't be nervous. My brother is obsessed with you. But, like, in a good way. I truly believe that the reason he has never settled down was because he was waiting for someone like you to come along." She smiles softly. "You guys are great together and I'm just glad to get a front-row seat to your lives colliding." She pauses and searches my expression. "So, let's focus on what we need to do first. What time will the storm shelter guys be here?"

"Around 8:30 is what they told me."

"Good. I can't wait to see it after work. Take a picture of the kids inside and share it on Facebook so the community can see what they helped with."

"I will, promise." I say, leaning in and hugging Avery. "Thank you for everything. You are such a good friend and you are exactly who I needed today. I know everything will be fine. Your brother is a good man and I truly believe he and I are meant to be together. I think I'm just a little nervous about taking this next step."

"That's normal." She says with a soft smile. "Your last relationship ended in a lot of heartache. The person who you trusted with your heart did not take care of it and it's difficult to just come back from that. But you can't let that keep you from the life and the love that you deserve."

* * *

"Say bologna sandwich!" I call out to the kids as they sit happily in the storm shelter, perched along benches lining the walls.

"Bologna sandwich!" The crew of kids call out, holding the suckers given to them by the storm shelter installation men on their way out the door. I snap a few photos of the kids and then instruct them to head into the backyard so we can have our afternoon recess time.

While keeping one eye on the kids, I edit the photo, covering their faces for privacy's sake and post it on my Facebook page, thanking the community for their contribution to my business. I finish and tuck my phone away in my pocket just as Ava makes her way through the gate into the backyard.

"Hey!" I say with a smile. "You need to go inside and see the shelter. It's amazing."

"I will in just a second, I promise. I have been cleaning and painting next door all day and I am just ready to be around another human being for a minute." She says with a laugh. "I'm so excited the shelter is all done, though."

"Me too." I nod. "Plus, that means that you and Piper will have a place to come hang out during storms, too. No more going to the church and sitting on the floor of the crowded basement."

"What? And pass up sitting next to someone's dog even though the sign clearly says no pets allowed? Or sit across from someone who won't stop coughing? Where will I catch a virus?"

I raise a brow. "Or where will you meet hot single dads?"

She blushes. "That too. I haven't seen him much since then. Just in passing when we come to get the kids."

"I can find a way to make you run into each other. I wouldn't mind playing matchmaker."

"Absolutely not. I don't need anyone playing cupid with me." She says with a laugh. "If it's meant to be, it'll happen."

I raise a brow at my friend. "You can't say you're leaving it up to fate, but then never put yourself out there to let fate do its job."

"Mom, are you here to pick me up?" Piper asks, running across the yard towards the area where the two of us stand, interrupting my lecture.

"Hi, sweet girl. Well, I actually just came outside to clean my paint brushes and came to say hi. Are you ready to leave? Either way is fine with me."

Piper ponders the question. "Are we going to paint my room today?"

"We can if you want to."

"Then yes. I want to get my room painted so I can decorate it and have Kate over for a sleepover really soon."

"Sounds like you have some work to do today, then." Ava says with a smile before turning back to me. "I guess we are heading home for the day."

"You're brave, letting her help you paint." I say with a laugh as Piper runs off to tell her friends goodbye.

Ava waves me off. "She'll lose interest pretty quickly, I think. Plus, her carpet is going to need to be replaced anyway so a little paint won't hurt. Then I won't be the bad guy for not letting her help."

"I can't wait to see the finished product." I say with a laugh. "What color did she pick?"

Ava shakes her head. "Pistachio green. She's such a weird kid."

"Weird kids are the best kind."

* * *

The rest of the day passes quickly and I'm working on doing my last bit of cleaning after the kids leave, when there's a knock at the door.

I stand on tiptoe to check the peephole and find Bryan

187

standing on the other side.

"Hey, you." I say with a smile as I open the door. I know it really has only been a couple of weeks since I last saw him, but it feels like a lifetime. All the feelings of anxiety I've had about this moment all day are already melting away. Nothing feels weird. This just feels right. As though it's something we've done all along. "Already done moving in?"

Bryan, still holding me in a tight bear hug, leans down to kiss the top of my head while it rests on his chest. "Oh yeah, it took no time once the guys got to the house. We really just had to unload my tools and my gun safe. I've never been so happy to have bought all new furniture. I just gave everything else away to the other guys in my unit before I left town."

I laugh. "I'm glad you did, too. Truthfully, I take great pride in being the only woman to be in that bed."

"The only one welcome in my bed for the rest of my life." He says, leaning in close to kiss me. "You are my home and I'm so glad to finally be here with you."

"Me too."

And despite all my fear about today, I mean it. This is exactly where I want to be. For once, I feel like I'm where I belong.

Chapter 23

"Mom! Can we feed the ducks?" Kate asks, running across the grassy lawn of the zoo and stopping in front of me. "Please?"

I frown and dig around inside my purse. "Kate, I don't actually think I have any change on me." I say, eyeing the nearby gumball machine that's used to sell duck food to zoo goers. "I totally forgot to get some quarters out of my change jar before we left."

"Aw man!" Kate sulks. "Do we have any change in the car? I might have a quarter under my booster seat." She offers.

"Hey, I have you covered." Bryan laughs, digging in his pocket. "I have two quarters right here. Let's go get you ladies some duck food."

The girls don't waste another second, barreling towards the wooden dock where the duck food machine is waiting for them, causing Bryan to jog in order to catch up with them. I laugh and shake my head, but take my time joining them. This has been one of the best days the kids and I have had in a while.

In fact, every day since Bryan moved has been pretty incredible. Sure, I've still been busy working during the day and the girls keep me busy enough in the evening, but there's been something comforting about having Bryan nearby. Even if it's just someone to help me clean up from dinner or to help the girls practice for the tee ball and softball teams. For being just a couple of people that have only been dating for a couple of months, I feel like we have more family time than I've ever had before. Today is the perfect example of this.

We started the day off by driving half an hour away to Independence for a low-key day of fun. After a quick stop at the coffee shop, Highroad, we took our lattes (and chocolate milk for the girls) and started our trek around the zoo. The Independence Zoo isn't large by any stretch of the imagination, but it's the perfect size for a quick family outing. After seeing the monkeys at monkey island, the reptiles, the bears and the peacocks, it feels nice to sit down on a bench and watch as the girls feed the ducks. Bryan finishes getting the girls their duck food and joins me.

"Man, it's been forever since I was here." He says, shaking his head. "Probably the last time was a field trip in elementary school. It's funny though, because not much has changed."

I reach over and squeeze his hand. "I love this place. It definitely helps that it's free to get in and it's just big enough to cover everything and be home before dinner. I bring the kids here a lot. I've even brought my daycare kids, too. We're lucky to have it."

Bryan puts his hand over his stomach. "Speaking of dinner. We should have packed a lunch. I'm getting hungry."

"I have some snacks in my bag." I offer.

"I was thinking Dairy Queen, actually." Bryan laughs. "I haven't had it in years."

"I could go for a burger and a blizzard right now. Girls, are you about ready for lunch?" I ask calling out to them.

"Wait!" Kenzi yells, running towards us, with her hands up. "Can we ride the train first? Just one time."

"Of course we can ride the train." Bryan answers for me, pushing his hands on his knees to stand up. "But only if we go right now. Otherwise, I might get so hungry I'll have to go fight a duck for his food."

"Oh, no!" Kenzi says with a giggle as she shakes her head. "Not the duck food. That's yucky."

"Welp, we better go ride the train and then go get some lunch then." I say, pulling a baby wipe from my bag and handing it to Kenzi. "Speaking of, clean the duck food off your hands." I tell her as Kate joins us and I hand her a baby wipe, too. "Kate, let's go ride the train and then get some lunch. Sound good to you?"

"Yes! I'm starving." Kate agrees, nodding happily, as she finishes wiping her hands. She throws the used wipe in a nearby trash can before turning back to us. "Thank you for bringing us here today. It was a lot of fun." She says, before leaning in to hug Bryan around the waist.

I watch as Bryan's face softens as he receives the hug. "You're welcome, kiddo." He says, grinning as Kenzi can't help herself by joining in on the hug party. Bryan turns his head to face me. "You feeling left out over there?" He asks with a wink.

"Maybe a little." I admit, as he reaches out an arm and pulls me in close to the rest of them.

"Yay! Family hug!" Kenzi shouts with glee as she wraps an arm around my body and squeezes all of us.

I pause, bracing myself for Kate to interject, but, to my surprise, she doesn't. Finally, the sound of a stomach growling interrupts the moment. All of us begin to laugh.

"Who was that?" Kate asks, darting our eyes between the three of us.

"Not me." Kenzi shakes her head.

"Me neither." I reply, looking at Bryan.

"Listen, I told you guys I was starving." Bryan quickly defends himself. "I wasn't kidding about stealing the duck food."

"Well, sounds like we need to go get that train ride out of the way so we can feed this guy." I say to the girls as I stand from my seat. "You wanna race?"

Without even as much as an answer, both girls take off toward the kiddie train. A small wooden fifteen car train that travels along a track circling the park next to the zoo. Bryan and I follow their lead, taking off after them.

"I win!" I hear Kate scream, as she reaches the gate to form a line for the train.

"Second!" Kenzi reports as she reaches her sister.

Bryan and I slow to a jog as we join the girls. Just as we reach our stopping point and catch our breath, I hear a word that makes my skin crawl.

"Daddy!" Kenzi cries out in excitement.

I pause, hoping that she's mistaken, or trying out a very inappropriate and way too early nickname for Bryan. But alas, I'm wrong. I watch as Ben and Amber approach to join us in line. Amber is wearing a baby carrier on her chest, with a bald headed baby boy tucked away inside. Well, it was a great day. Until now.

"Hi, my beautiful girls." Ben says, bending down to hug Kenzi and then Kate. "What a surprise to see you here." He says, shifting his eyes to Bryan and myself.

"Hi." I mutter to him, trying my best to resist being annoyed but failing. Why in the world did he have to show up and ruin our great day? And if I had to see him, why did I have to see her, too? Ugh.

"I like your baby," Kenzi says, standing on tiptoe to admire the little person swaddled against Amber's chest.

"Oh thank you," Amber says, squatting down to talk to my daughter. "His name is Henry."

"Aw, he's so cute," Kenzi says, gently patting his back.

Amber darts her eyes to Ben and stands to face him. "Did you not tell the girls about him?"

Ben shoves his hands in his pockets and lowers his voice. "Well, no, not yet."

Now Amber looks angry, and I love it. "Are you kidding me? He's six months old. Is this why you haven't wanted them to meet him? Because they didn't know he existed?"

"This really isn't the right place for this conversation." Ben argues.

"Well, then let's go find the right place." Amber says, crossing her arms in front of her chest just as the train pulls up.

The conductor, wearing a name tag that says Crystal, works to get the previous crowd unloaded and then opens the gate for us.

"Girls, we will see you later, okay? We are going to skip the train ride."

Kate furrows her brow. "Why? Please ride the train with us."

"Yeah, Dad. It'll be so fun. It'll be all of our family on the train at once," Kenzi adds.

I bite my tongue to keep myself from saying something I shouldn't.

Ben turns to me and I shrug. He turns to Amber, who rolls her eyes. "Whatever. Let's ride the train, then." She says, storming past him and taking a seat behind Kate and Kenzi, who are already seated.

Bryan and I exchange a look and then sit down in front of the girls.

"Everyone ready?" The conductor asks, turning to check on us.

"Yes!" we reply, some more chipper than others.

"Wait!" Kate exclaims, holding up her hands. "We need a picture."

I raise a brow and turn to face her. "A picture?"

"Yes! Please mom?" Kate whines. "We need a picture of all of us together. I want to keep it forever."

"I'll take it for you!" Crystal offers, holding out a hand for a phone.

I force a smile and fork over my device.

"Say Choo-choo!" The conductor says.

"Choo-Choo." We reply, posing for the photo.

She hands the phone back to me. "Make sure those are good." She says. "I took a few."

Quickly, I swipe through. "Yep, looks great. Thank you." I say.

"Have her send that to you so I can put it on my Instagram." I hear Amber whisper to Ben.

My eyes widen, and I look up at Bryan. He wraps an arm around me and squeezes me tight, kissing the side of my head, just as the train jolts to begin its journey.

I turn to check on the girls, who are seated together, looking over their respective sides at the park as it moves by.

"This is so cool," Kate says dreamily as she waves to a little girl who is making her way into the park.

"Yeah. Cool." Mimics Kenzi as she smiles up at her big sister.

I let my eyes wander back to Ben and Amber. Ben is staring

back at me, specifically at Bryan's arm around me. Amber is staring up the side of Ben's head, completely unnoticed. I turn back towards Bryan and snuggle in closer to him. "This is so freaking awkward." I mutter into his ear. "I'm sorry."

"It's fine." He chuckles. "I knew I'd have to deal with your ex, eventually. I'm not afraid of him."

"I'm not either. Just annoyed." I mumble.

"Screw 'em. We are happy and that's all that matters."

* * *

"Wait! Don't come in yet!" Kate screams, as I round the corner into the living room.

After our trip to the zoo today, we came home and finally relaxed a bit. There's something comforting about knowing that, Bryan won't have to leave to drive back to Texas today.

I freeze in place, right inside the kitchen. "Why not?" I ask, not daring to move an inch.

"Because I'm doing something. It's a surprise. Just wait. Please?" She begs.

I let out an audible sigh. "Okay, I guess I'll just banish myself to the kitchen then."

"Okay, bye." Kenzi pipes up, just as the two of them erupt into giggles.

"Should I be worried?" I ask, still not daring to enter the room.

"No, but I should be." Bryan responds with a groan.

"Shhh. Don't talk, you might mess up your hair."

"How can I mess up my hair by talking?"

"You just could!" Kenzi argues. "Kenzi, are you almost

done?"

"Yep!" Kenzi replies. "Just one more nail." She adds. "And done!"

"Okay mom, you can come see now!" Kate calls out from the living room.

I enter my living room and can't believe my eyes. Bryan is seated on the floor. Both girls are standing next to him, with proud grins, arms open wide, Vanna style.

"Isn't he beautiful?" Kate asks proudly.

"Um, yes. The most beautiful." I agree with a laugh. "Did you paint his nails?" I inquire, moving closer to inspect Bryan's new pink and purple nail polish that is smeared on his nails and most of his fingers as well.

"Yes! I'm going to be a beauty shop girl when I grow up." Kenzi reports proudly. "Just like Sierra."

"Well." I say, lowering Bryan's hand that I'm holding. "I think you'll do a great job at it. This is a real promising start. And Kate, I've never seen his hair so beautiful. I see you even added some butterfly claw clips to his beard."

"Because he's extra fancy." She reports, proudly.

"Well, you guys better let me get a picture of all of you together before Bryan has to leave to head home." I say with a smirk. "Just in case I need blackmail one day."

Bryan offers me an exaggerated grin and both girls move in to stand proudly next to him. I snap a few photos and then tuck my phone away in my pocket. "Okay, ladies. It's time for the two of you to get through showers and your bedtime routine."

"But it's summer." Kate whines.

"It sure is." I confirm. "But we still have daycare kids coming tomorrow. So, we have to stay in our routine."

"Fine." Kate grumbles and turns towards Bryan, hugging

his side. "Thanks for letting me do your hair. You can keep the clips if you want to." She says solemnly.

"Oh, that's so nice of you." He chuckles in return. "Thanks. I'll bring them back next time I come to visit."

"Will it be soon?" Kenzi asks, now hugging his other side. "You're so fun."

"Yes, it'll be soon. I promise. Probably tomorrow, if your mom doesn't mind." He says, hugging them both back. "But for now, I gotta go so you can get to bed."

Kenzi pauses and then lurches forward to hug him one more time. "I wish you could just live here. I like it when you're here."

I pause and look at my girls. "You do, huh?"

Both kids nod happily.

"We love Bryan." Kenzi says, still hanging on to him.

"I love you guys, too. But you still have to get ready for bed." He answers, untangling Kenzi from his neck.

"You heard the guy. Move." I tell them, pointing down the hall.

The girls nod and turn towards their rooms. "Bye." They groan as they disappear down the hall.

Once they are gone, Bryan and I lock eyes. His heart obviously melted into a puddle of goo. I reach over and pick up his hand to examine the manicure. "Luckily for you, this is washable nail polish. It'll come off in the shower. I never let them use the real stuff."

"Thank goodness." He laughs, using the hand I'm holding to pull me towards him. I crash into his chest with a thud. "Those girls are something else."

"Yeah, they are." I agree. "And they apparently really like you a lot." I add, not mentioning Kenzi's profession of love.

"I really like them, too." He whispers, leaning his forehead against mine. "Their mom isn't so bad, either."

I lean up on tiptoe to lightly kiss his lips. "Their mom is kind of a handful sometimes."

"Good." He says, reaching around to grab me from behind. "My hands are always looking for something to grab on to." He mutters before leaning down to kiss me again. This time, taking his time to kiss me slowly, and with more pressure than before.

"Alright Casanova. You better get going before we have questions to answer." I say, gently pushing him away. "I'll talk to you tomorrow."

"See you then."

Chapter 24

"Alright Kate. You've got this!" I yell to my daughter as she walks up to home plate.

"Oh my gosh, she looks so cute in her little uniform." Avery gushes. "I'm so excited to see her play."

Ball season is in full swing and both of the girls have been keeping us busy with their practice schedule. Not surprisingly, Kenzi decided rather quickly that she wasn't actually interested in playing tee ball. Instead, she would prefer to practice her cartwheels and pick dandelions. At least she's cute when she's running around the field in her oversized helmet.

Kate, however, has loved every second of practice and invited everyone to her first game. And I mean everyone. By the time the game is starting, my lawn chair, which I placed along the fence line near third base, is surrounded by our friends and family. Bryan, Avery, Juliet, Ava, Piper, Becca, Nathan and my parents all came out to sit with Kenzi and me while we watch my girls' first game.

"Eye on the ball, Kate! You've got this!" my ex-husband shouts out over the crowd from his seat on the bleachers. Ugh. And yes, of course he's here with Amber and their baby.

At the sound of Ben's voice, Ava and I look at each other and roll our eyes. Yes, I am thankful that Ben is involved. The girls are lucky to have a dad that loves them and spends time with them and makes time to come to their events. I just wish I didn't have to see him while he does it.

"Good swing!" Bryan calls out to Kate as she just barely misses the first pitch.

"Just a little sooner!" Ben adds.

I turn to look at him, just as his son, who is in Amber's arms, pulls off Ben's hat and throws it under the bleachers to reveal that Ben is balding. Quickly, might I add. I elbow Ava and motion towards my ex's receding hairline as he attempts to rescue his hat from the sunflower seed covered dirt.

"Is he going bald?" Ava whispers, in an attempt to not giggle.

"It sure seems that way, doesn't it?"

"Karma," is all Ava says in return. "The only thing better would be if Kate hits a home run and smashes his truck windshield."

"Maybe one day."

* * *

"Great work out there, kid," Nathan says to Kate after the game as she makes her way towards her awaiting fan club.

Derek, who is on patrol, came out to the ball field to walk through and steal a glance at Kate's game, offers her a high five. "Kate, you have an arm like a rocket. I'm impressed."

Kate's face turns red, and she smiles brightly. "Thank you." She says to Derek before turning to look at me. "Mom, that was so much fun. I can't wait for my next game."

"You did great." I tell her, wrapping her into a hug, as she runs over to tell her dad and Amber hello.

"She's going to be so much fun to watch as she gets older." Bryan tells me. "I can't believe she had never played before."

I shake my head. "Not even tee ball. I just never assumed she'd be interested in something like this." I pause to think. "Or maybe it's because I had never been interested in sports, so I didn't think to ask if she wanted to play."

"Well, either way, she's into them now and that's all that matters."

"Mom, can we go out for ice cream? My team is going since we won." Kate asks, running back towards us.

"Yes, of course. Tell everyone bye and thank them for coming and we will get you some ice cream. You deserve it."

Within ten minutes, Kenzi, Bryan and I are sitting at a picnic table outside The Burger Shack, while Kate sits with her team nearby.

"Mom." says Kenzi, while eating her soft serve cone. "I don't think I'm a baseballer after all."

I nod. "That's okay. You never know if you'll like something until you try it. You do need to finish out the season since you started it, but then you don't have to play again next year. What do you think you'd like to try next?"

She ponders the question for a moment, tapping her finger on her ice cream covered chin before speaking again. "Maybe dance? Like Piper does? I'm a very good twirler."

I crack a smile. Of course, my two girls would settle on two completely different hobbies.

"We can try it. We can sign you up for a class when the new school year starts. I bet they do tumbling, too."

"So, I could do cartwheels, too?"

"I think so."

"Bryan, can we come to your house tomorrow so we can

201

practice batting?" Kate asks, as she rushes towards our table. "And catching?"

"My house?" Bryan asks, raising a brow.

"Yeah, you have more room, and I'm probably going to knock the ball into outer space. Plus, you have a trampoline now, so we can use it when we get done."

"Yes! I can practice my tumbling." Kenzi squeals, standing to try out a few twirls with her half melted ice cream cone in her hand. "Please?" She begs, causing Kate to join her in the begging.

"Okay, yes. That's fine." Bryan says with a laugh. "As long as it's okay with mom."

I finish my cone and use my napkin to wipe my hands. "Works for me." I say with a shrug. "As long as you really don't mind us taking over your house."

Bryan leans across the table to kiss my lips. "Of course I want you taking over my house. I wouldn't have gotten your kids a trampoline if I didn't want you there."

"Okay, I just hope you don't regret this."

"I will never regret spending time with you guys." He smiles, squeezing my hand before picking it up to kiss it.

"Cringe." groans Kate. "Grownups who kiss are so gross."

Better get used to it, kid.

* * *

"You guys go ahead. I'll be right out there." I say, as Bryan and the girls head out back for batting and jumping practice.

I creep to the window overlooking the backyard and as soon as I see they are occupied; I tiptoe out the front door to my van.

As quietly as possible, I sneak around to the back of the van where I left the housewarming gift I brought for Bryan. When we arrived, after unloading the kids, I put the cow canvas I painted against the back of my van. Out of sight, but easy for me to sneak outside and grab. I didn't want to have to close a door, causing him to hear me getting it out of the van later.

Once the piece of art is secured under my arm, I sneak back into the house. Stopping to ensure they are still outside, I dash into Bryan's bedroom and place the canvas on his dresser, ensuring it overlooks his bed. I want this to be the first thing he sees when he wakes up in the morning, or when he lays down for bed tonight.

Satisfied with my placement, I close the door and sneak outside to enjoy some time with my girls and my boyfriend. Anxiously awaiting the discovery.

* * *

Bryan: Madison, what the hell did you leave in my bedroom?

I roll over in my bed and check the text that just came through on my phone from Bryan before erupting into giggles. The girls and I have only been home from Bryan's for about an hour. We spent all day there playing outside, eating dinner and vegging out with a movie. Now we are all showered and getting ready for bed after a long, fun day.

Madison: You mean the priceless piece of art I left you? I can't believe it took you this long to find it, honestly.
  Bryan: Yeah, well after you guys left, I might have fallen

asleep in my recliner. I just got up to drag myself to get into the shower when I found myself face to face with a deranged linebacker cow in my bedroom. I almost had a heart attack.

Madison: I don't know why you're so surprised. I told you I was going to gift it to you.

Bryan: Well, if it means that much to you, I'll find it a prominent space in the house. Maybe on the mantle.

Madison: No really, feel free to throw it away. Or burn it. I won't mind.

Bryan: Oh no. It's a gift, and I'd never throw away a gift. Just you wait and see.

Chapter 25

"Okay friends." I say, standing in the middle of the kitchen while I address the daycare kids. "As soon as you finish eating, I want you to put your plate on the counter and go change into your swimsuits and water shoes. If you need help, let me know and I will help you."

Just then, Bryan enters the room wearing a pair of grey swim trunks and a black t-shirt. "Aw, I didn't know I could ask for help to get ready." He teases, before shooting me a wink and joining me next to the counter. "What can I do to help?" He asks, as the kids one by one stand from the table and bring me their empty plates.

I look around to assess the situation. "Why don't you work on loading the dishwasher and I will help get the kids ready?" I suggest. "Thanks for coming to help today. Even with Becca coming here in a bit, International Mud Day can get a little crazy, and the more adults on deck to help, the better."

Bryan shakes his head. "I still think you made up this whole holiday."

I scoff. "International Mud Day is a real thing! In fact, it's a big deal in the Early Childhood community." I say with a laugh. "And it's so fun. It's easily my favorite day of the entire year. I look forward to it every June."

Just then, the doorbell rings. "That's Miss Becca." I tell the kids, in a singsong voice. This results in most of them breaking out in cheers. I hustle to the living room and let her inside.

"Hey!" I say, welcoming her in. "Are you ready for a really fun day?"

"So ready." She confirms, as she picks up the clipboard next to the door and fills out her time sheet for the morning. She places her backpack on the bench by the front door. "I brought a change of clothes, too."

"Good idea." I laugh. "You'll need them."

"Miss Becca, are you ready to play in the mud with us?" Piper asks. "Can we play spa and give you a mud mask?"

Becca's eyes widen. "Um..." she begins, trying to stall her answer.

"Okay, this might be a good time for some ground rules. Everyone's eyes on me, please. Give me five."

The kids all turn to face me, holding a hand in the air to show they are paying attention.

"Okay, we went through and made sure the mud didn't have any rocks inside it, but you make sure you pay attention. Don't throw mud clumps at people, do not rub mud in someone's face. Rubbing it on yourself is fine, do not eat it, actually just don't put it in your mouth."

"Well, then, what can we do?" Carson asks.

"You can stomp in the mud, sit in it, cover yourself in it. The outdoor kitchen is available to make mud pies. You can use it as finger paint on the patio..." I pause for a second. "If you have any idea of something to do, and you wonder if you will get in trouble for doing it, ask. You are going to be so mad if you have to sit in time out and watch all of your friends having fun without you. Don't take the chance. Got it?"

"Got it." They respond in a chorus.

"Okay, well, let's get dressed and go play in the mud."

* * *

"You look like you need a hug," Bryan says, stalking his way towards me with his arms open wide. From the neck down, this man is completely covered in mud.

"Oh, I'm okay." I say, nervously stepping back to avoid his incoming grasp.

"Ohhh... Miss Madi wants hugs?" Piper squeals, approaching me from the left side.

"Oh mom. Do you want to cuddle?" Kate chimes in, making her way around me to approach me from the right.

"You guys. Don't you think I'm already muddy enough?"

"Nope!" Giggles Piper as she closes the distance between us and pounces on me, hugging me tightly.

Quickly, I lower myself to the ground and allow Kate, Kenzi, Julia and Carson to dogpile me. The entire group of kids erupts into giggles. Luckily, the rest of the crew is busy playing in the mud kitchen or they would be all over me, too.

I allow the kids to cover me in their excess mud for about a minute before I break it up. "Alright friends. That's enough mud wrestling." I say with a laugh. "Go play."

"Okay." They groan before climbing out of the pile and heading back to the mud pit. The mud pit that Bryan created for them this morning thanks to a water hose and several wheelbarrows full of mud from his house.

"Let's make a mud castle!" Piper announces as they make their way back to the pile.

"Okay!" Answers Kate.

I sneak over to Bryan, who is lost in his own world, staring at his phone. I approach him from the back and quietly lean down to wrap my mud covered arms around his neck. As soon as I make contact with him, he quickly closes the message tab he's in and drops his phone in his lap. Then, he turns his face towards mine, scratching at my face with his beard. "What're you doing?" He grumbles into my hair.

"Paying you back for the dog pile you got me involved in before leaving me all alone covered in children."

Bryan laughs. "I got a video of that so you can remember it forever." He says, opening the photos on his phone and showing me.

I watch the video and shake my head. "Bryan, I can't believe you threw me to the wolves like that." I tease. "Some prince charming you are." I say, just as a Facebook message notification from someone named Carrie slides down on the screen.

Carrie. Who the hell is Carrie? And why is my boyfriend secretly messaging a woman in the middle of the day, not twenty feet away from me?

I step back from Bryan, putting distance between us and fighting back the tears building in my eyes. Obviously this is the other shoe I was waiting on dropping. This is the Bryan that Avery thought her brother was all along and we were all just stupid that we believed he was a good one. And now, I've gotten hurt all over again.

However, I don't have any time to question him. Instead, I watch as one of the Fawn Creek Fire trucks pulls into the alley behind the house and comes to a stop.

Cody hops out of the truck and leans over the fence. "Hey,

I hear there are some muddy kids over here that might be interested in a sprinkler." He laughs, looking at my kiddos covered in mud staring at him.

I jog towards Cody. "Hey. Yes, they would love that. I totally forgot that I told you to come over." I say, looking at my watch. "And I forgot to tell my daycare parents a firetruck will be here. I better send them a text," I say, just as my phone rings in my hand. It's my mother.

"Hey, mom. What's up?" I ask.

"Madi, is everything okay?" She asks, sounding stressed. "I just got a call that there's a fire truck at your house."

I laugh. "Man, word travels fast in this town. I knew this was coming. It's International Mud Day. Cody is here to spray the kids with some water. He brought one of the little tanker trucks to do it."

"So, everything is okay?"

"We are great." I confirm. "I promise, but I need to get back to it."

"Okay, have fun."

"Oh, we will." I promise, as Cody finishes unraveling the hose from the truck.

"Hey guys!" He calls out to the kids, who have all gathered at the fence to watch him work. "Wanna play in a sprinkler?" He asks.

"A sprinkler?" Carson repeats. "What sprinkler?"

"This one!" Cody says, as he pulls open the latch and points the hose towards the sky.

Everyone immediately makes their way to the center of the yard to be under the falling sheet of water. And I mean everyone. Bryan, Becca and I join the kids for our water park addition to our mud day. We take turns holding hands with the kids, and spinning in circles, completely soaking ourselves with water.

"This is the best day ever!" Kate yells, with water dripping from her face.

"Yeah, it is." I agree. "Best day ever."

* * *

"Okay." I say, making my way into the kitchen, still towel drying my hair, but at least wearing some dry clothes. "Thanks for getting the plates ready while I changed, Becca."

"No problem." She answers cheerily.

"We have so much work cut out for us today during nap time." I tell her, eyeing my laundry room that is currently covered in wet clothes and discarded beach towels.

"Well, if you want to take over this, I can start a load of laundry." She suggests.

"That'd be great." I agree, already getting to work on making plates for the kids. The kids are sitting in the living room in dry clothes, watching an episode of Bluey while we work on getting ready for lunch.

I look at the counter and see Bryan's phone sitting there. It lights up with a notification that he's received a message. Again. Unfortunately for me, the notification doesn't tell me who the message is from.

I shake my head, trying to clear my thoughts and get to work on making plates. When he enters the room, he picks up his phone and clears the notifications before making his way towards me and kissing my forehead.

"Well, Freckles. That was a lot of fun today. I definitely thought you were crazy when you said we were going to play in the mud, but it was so fun."

"I'm glad you enjoyed it." I mutter, working on putting mixed fruit onto each plate, not even attempting to hide my annoyance.

His phone vibrates again, causing me to tense. As he opens the notification, I can't stop myself from sneaking a peek. Another message from Carrie. He quickly swipes it away and shoves his phone in his pocket.

That's all I can take today.

Where does this man get the audacity to stand in my house and text another woman? Ben might have made a fool out of me with his affair, but I will not allow it to happen again. I deserve better than this.

Of course, I can't even confront him. I have to remain calm for my kids because my tone sets the tone for the entire household.

Bryan turns to me. "Well, I have some things to go take care of if you're done with me for the day."

"Yeah. We've got it from here." I say, waving him off. "Have a good day. Thanks for your help." I say, before turning towards the living room. "Kids, it's time for lunch!"

The kids make their way towards the kitchen, nearly running over Bryan in the process and take their seats at the table.

Bryan kisses my cheek. "I'll text you later. Have a good rest of your day. Love you."

"Bye." I reply, busying myself with helping the kids get settled. I don't even turn to see if he's noticed that I didn't say I loved him back.

With tear-filled eyes, I wait as Bryan makes his way towards the living room and out the door before turning to look at Becca.

"You okay?" She asks, leaning against the doorway. A look

of concern is apparent on her face.

I shake my head. "I'm fine. Sorry. Okay friends, let's pray so we can dig in."

* * *

"Have a good weekend!" I call out to Carson and Eric as they make their way out the front door, just as my phone buzzes on the end table. I lean over to check the notification and I'm not surprised to find that it's Bryan again.

Bryan: Do you want to come over for dinner tonight? I'll cook.

I swipe the notification away without opening the message. While yes, I'd love an excuse to get out of cooking tonight, even that won't convince me to see him right now.

Not when that man was standing in my house today texting another woman. I mean, it's disgusting enough that he is juggling me and at least one other person, but to do it in my house? And then look me in the eye like he did nothing wrong? Absolutely not.

Maybe I really am better off alone. Maybe I should follow Ava's lead and focus on my life instead of worrying about dating. I mean, out of all the men I had run in with since my divorce was finalized, Bryan was the only one that seemed worthwhile. If he isn't going to be the man I need, then maybe I don't need anyone at all.

This explains why he's been single for all this time. Why he's never been married and why Avery hated him for so long. He is not who I thought he was, and it's obviously best if I just cut my losses. It's too bad I let the kids get close to him. They love him and it's going to hurt when they find out he won't be coming around anymore. But kids are resilient, right? Isn't that what everyone always says?

I shake my head and stare at the space above the television in my living room. Maybe I need to get my mind off of things.

Just then, a knock at the door interrupts me. I move towards the door and check the peephole to find Avery on the other side.

"Hey." I say, pulling the door open, just as she pulls a bottle of wine from behind her back and presents it to me. "What's this for?"

"For you." She shrugs.

"But why?"

"Just for being who you are. The kids had so much fun today. Juliet has been chattering since I picked her up about making mud pies and splashing in mud puddles. I truly believe today was the best day of her life." She says, shaking her head. "And all it took was a little bit of dirt and water. Plus, a really good teacher."

I blush. "It was a fun day. I loved seeing the kids go crazy and enjoy getting dirty." I admit. "Kids learn through play, and it's just up to me to come up with ways to keep it exciting for them."

"See? And this is why we are lucky to have you. Because you care. You're not in this to collect a check and do the bare minimum. You are amazing and we love you, and I just hope you always know how thankful we are for you." She says with a grin. "And now you're dating my brother and dare I say things are getting pretty serious there?"

I frown. Avery is the last person in the world I want to talk to about this, so instead, I lie. "Yeah, I think so."

"Well, I hope you guys are in this for the long haul because the only thing better than having you as Juliet's teacher will be to have you as her aunt, too."

I pause and swallow hard. "Avery, I don't know. It's kinda soon to talk about all that."

"Maybe, for regular people." She shrugs. "But the two of you are obviously made to be together. I think this thing is going to last a long time, friend." She beams before leaning in to hug me. "Anyway, enjoy the wine and your night. I'm going to get back home and make dinner. Derek is there with Juliet now, so I could run to the liquor store."

"Thank you." I say, admiring the wine bottle in my hand. "And it's a screw top, so I don't have to ask someone to help me open it." I laugh. "I can never get the cork out without ruining it."

"Well, I'm sure my brother would come help anytime." She says with a wink.

"I'm sure he would."

Here and everywhere else in town, too.

* * *

I'm just finishing loading the dishwasher with the plates from dinner when my phone vibrates once again, this time with a phone call from Bryan.

I roll my eyes and lean over to silence it. I'm still not in the mood to talk to him. As soon as the ringing stops, another text comes through.

214

Bryan: Hey, I'm not sure what I did wrong, but can you at least message me back and let me know you're okay?

Madison: I'm okay. Just not feeling well.

Bryan: Oh no. I'm sorry. What can I do? Can I bring you some dinner? Or some medicine?

Madison: No, I'm fine. I probably just picked up a bug from one of the kids. I'm going to get the girls in bed and lay down to sleep it off.

Bryan: Just let me know if anything changes, okay? I can be there in a heartbeat. And keep your notifications on tonight. The weather could get dicey.

Madison: Thanks. I will.

Bryan: At least you have a storm shelter you can get in, right at the house while you're feeling bad.

Yeah. At least I have that.

Chapter 26

After getting the girls settled into bed, I lay down on the couch with the news on, and prepare for a long evening of watching the radar. Again. This seems to be my every night routine now that storm season is in full swing.

I must have drifted off to sleep while the news was on, because the next thing I know, I wake up to the sound of a loud pounding at the door.

After unraveling myself from the blankets on the couch, I finally jump up and check the peephole to find Ava and Piper on my porch. I open the door and usher them inside.

"Hey." she says, placing Piper on the floor. "Have you been watching the radar?"

"No, I guess I fell asleep." I admit, just as the sound of the city tornado siren begins to blare. My eyes widen.

"Looks like it's time to try out that storm shelter of yours." Ava says, eyeing Piper nervously.

"I'll get the girls. You guys go on and get inside the shelter." I tell her, already rushing towards the kids' rooms. "Kate, wake up. We have to go get in the storm shelter."

Kate sits up groggily and rubs her eyes. "What? Why? Are we going to have a tornado?"

I bite my lip, trying to hide my anxiety. "No, baby. We will be okay, but we are going to go get in the shelter just in case. Piper and her mommy are already out there." I tell her, as I rush into Kenzi's room. "Hi, baby." I say softly, lifting her from her bed and cuddling her close. "We're going to go get in the storm shelter." I tell her. "Let's go."

Without another word, the girls and I make our way towards the garage and find Ava and Piper sitting along the wood bench waiting for us.

"Welcome." Ava says wearily, forcing her best smile.

I close the door and look around the space and at our tired kiddos. "Girls, why don't I unroll the sleeping bag and you can all lie down there while we wait this thing out?" I don't wait for an answer before getting to work at constructing the makeshift pallet. I unroll the sleeping bag and lay it in the space on the floor before adding a couple of pillows for the girls to lie on. Dutifully, the kids lay down and I cover them with a blanket. Then I hand them a tablet and tell Kate to pull up a movie while we wait.

Once the kids are settled, I take a seat next to Ava. "Well, I'm glad one of us was watching the weather. I can't believe I fell asleep." I say, shaking my head. "It's been a long day."

Ava frowns and looks back at the kids before looking at me. "Hey, it's okay. Us single moms have to stick together. They say it takes a village, don't they?"

I nod. "Indeed, they do."

"I'm surprised Bryan wasn't here, to be honest. I would have just assumed that he would have come over once there was a threat of bad weather."

I frown. "Shit. Bryan." I say, pulling my phone from my pocket. "He's probably been blowing my phone up. I've had it on do not disturb." I whisper.

However, once I check my notifications, I have nothing from him. "That's weird. He hasn't messaged me." I say, quickly opening my phone contacts and firing off a text to him.

Madison: Are you awake?

Ava raises a brow. "Why was your phone on 'do not disturb'?"

I shake my head. "It's a long story. I'll tell you in a minute." I scroll to his name on my phone and attempt to call him. The call fails immediately. No service.

I turn to Ava. "I'm going to step outside to call Bryan and make sure he's taking shelter too."

As I step into the garage, the call finally connects.

Bryan answers groggily. "Hello? Are you okay, Freckles?"

"Are you sleeping?"

"I was. You guys wore me out today. What's wrong?"

"What's wrong?" I repeat. "What's wrong is there is a tornado siren going off and you are in a manufactured home. You need to get in your storm shelter."

"My phone didn't go off or anything." Bryan mumbles, the sound of his voice moving away further.

"The siren is going off here. We are in our shelter now. You need to go." I command.

"Headed that way now. I won't have any service down there, so I'll text you after. Bye. I love you."

"Love you, too."

After hanging up the phone, I make my way back into the safe room.

The girls are snuggled together on the floor, half asleep, watching their movie.

I plop down next to Ava and place my phone at my side.

"Okay, spill it." she says, eyeing me. "What happened with Bryan? It was going so well."

I shrug. "There's not much to tell. I caught him texting a woman named Carrie a few times today."

"About what?"

I shrug. "I don't know. Anytime I was close to him, he closed the messages."

She frowns. "Did you ask him about it?"

"No."

"So, you are assuming the worst?"

I let out a heavy sigh. "Can you blame me? Men don't have a great track record with me these days."

Ava shakes her head. "That just doesn't sound like something Bryan would do."

"I didn't think it was something Ben would do either." I argue. "But he did. The paternity test proved it."

"I just think you shouldn't jump to conclusions. There's probably a reasonable explanation for all of this. He loves you, Madi. I'm sure this is just some misunderstanding and you need to talk to him about it."

"Or maybe he's just too good to be true."

* * *

"Bye." I say, waving to Ava and Piper as they cross the yard back towards their house. "See you girls in a few hours."

"We might just sleep the day away." Ava laughs. "We will see how it goes, but if you don't see us, you'll know why."

"I'd do the same if I could. Night!" I call back to her before turning to walk back into the house. Both girls have already made a beeline to my bed and are snuggled under my blankets.

I check my watch. It's three in the morning. In three hours, my alarm will go off and I'll have a house full of kids to take care of not long after that. Not to mention the fact that all of those kids were ripped from their beds in the middle of the night to shelter from a tornado. Everyone will be on edge today. And it's my job to be the calm in the storm. How am I supposed to do that when I have my own storm to weather?

* * *

The sound of the alarm clock on my phone buzzes and wakes me from my slumber. Quickly, I grab the phone from the nightstand and silence it before checking in on the girls still sleeping soundly next to me. I rub my eyes and stare at the ceiling. I'm not ready for today.

It's rare that I wish I had a regular job. One with vacation days and sick days. A job where I could call in sick if I'm not feeling well or maybe call in late because I was awake until three in the morning sitting in a storm shelter with my kids and my neighbor. But, alas, I don't have that kind of job. If I don't clock in for the day, then all of my daycare parents miss work, too. It's not just about me, no matter how tired I am.

So instead, I have to deal with things the way I have been doing for the last year. One step at a time.

I let out a deep yawn and shuffle to the kitchen to start the coffee pot. After filling the reservoir with water, I pick up the can of coffee grounds and frown at the lightness of it.

Opening the lid confirms my suspicion. I'm out of coffee. I

don't have enough to make a cup, much less the pot that I need. Or let's face it, several pots that I will need to get through this day.

I could wait and ask a daycare parent to bring me coffee. I know they would. Avery and Ava make a habit of bringing me a coffee from time to time just to say thank you. But I will not make it until they show up. Even a can of Diet Dr. Pepper won't get me through this morning.

I make my way back towards my room and stick my head in the doorway.

"Hey girls." I say, moving towards the bed. I gently shake Kate and then Kenzi.

"I don't want to get up yet," Kate whines, hiding her head under the blanket.

"Not even for donuts?" I ask, hoping the prospect of a sugary breakfast will be enough for her.

"Donuts?!" she says, sitting up quickly in bed.

I laugh. "Yes. Donuts. Let's get your sister up and make a run to the coffee shop."

"Can I wear my pajamas?" Kate asks, already climbing out of bed.

"Absolutely." I say, lifting Kenzi from the bed, gently waking her. "Whatever it takes to get mama some coffee."

Chapter 27

"Good morning!" Cassidy cheerily calls out from behind the counter of Drip. "What a treat to see you three today. I usually only get to see you on the weekend."

I laugh as I guide the girls towards the donut counter. "Well, usually our mornings are pretty busy, but I forgot I emptied my coffee can yesterday. And after hunkering down from the storm warning last night, I was not about to go without caffeine today."

"Oh, man." Cassidy shakes her head, causing her curly blonde ponytail to shake wildly behind her head. "That storm sure was something. I hear some people on the edge of town got quite a bit of storm damage. The police chief was just in here telling me about it. Did Bryan get any damage?"

Bryan.

I haven't talked to him since we got in the shelter last night. Surely he's okay, right? I pull out my phone and fire off a text to him.

Madison: Did you survive the storm?

Then I turn back to my girls. "Ladies, have you chosen your donuts?"

The girls give Cassidy their order, both pink sprinkle donuts, and I order a large caramel latte.

Cassidy nudges her head towards the boutique wall in the cafe. "Hey, I just ordered bags of coffee from a local roaster, if you want to make sure you have enough to make it through the day."

I turn and make a beeline towards the coffee display to study the assortment. I pick up a bag of freshly ground coffee and examine it. Deciding after the past couple of days I've had, I deserve a treat. I carry the bag towards the counter and hand it to Cassidy. "Sold. I rarely spend this much on coffee for myself. Just as a gift for others." I admit. "But today it feels worth it."

"You'll probably never be able to drink the cheap stuff again." She warns me with a laugh, as she finishes making my drink. "But it's worth every penny."

"Well." I say, pushing my debit card across the counter. "At least that's one upside to being the only adult in the house. A bag of coffee will last me quite a while when I'm the only one drinking it."

Cassidy chuckles. "Not if a certain bearded man is there helping you." She says with a wink.

"Oh, right." I say. There's no way I'm going to talk to her about what's happening between us. At least not right now. "Okay, ladies. We need to head back home so we can be ready for our friends to show up."

Without an argument, the girls with their half eaten donuts make their way towards the door. "Bye Cassidy. Have a good day!" I call back. "And thanks for the caffeine."

"Anytime, sweetheart!" She replies.

I load the girls in the van and then get in myself before checking my phone. Still no response from Bryan. I turn to look at the girls. "We have a little bit of extra time. I'm going to take us on a small detour first."

"What's a detour?" asks Kenzi.

"A long boring drive." Kate replies.

I snicker. "It means that we are still going where we planned to go, but we are going to take the long way there. I just want to see if Bryan's house did okay in the storm last night."

"Why don't you just call and ask him?" Kate suggests.

I frown. "Well, I sent him a text, and he didn't answer. I just want to make sure he is okay." I say, keeping my eyes on the road.

Kate doesn't respond, which tells me she is satisfied enough with my answer. Or she's busy eating her donut and dropping crumbs all over my car.

I reach over and turn on the radio to fill the silence in the car and hopefully avoid any further questions.

Within no time, I'm turning off the highway onto a gravel road that leads me by Bryan's house. I should probably keep going. After all, I'm the one avoiding him. I'm the one that doesn't want to talk. But something in my gut says to turn down his driveway. All I have to do is get down there and look around to ensure his house is still standing. Hopefully, he's sleeping and won't even notice me.

Slowly, I make my way up the long gravel drive. However, once I round the corner my breath hitches.

Bryan's house is fine. It's still standing. Aside from the leaves all over the porch it looks like it didn't even storm there. But, around the back of the house, something is out of place. As I drive closer, I can see a large branch laying across the top of the in-ground storm shelter.

Shit. What if Bryan is stuck inside?

Quickly, I park the car in the front yard, using the house to shield the girls from the fallen tree. I turn to face the girls. "Do not move. Do not get out of this van. I'll be right back." I say, sternly.

The girls nod in agreement, and I jump out of the car, making my way around to the back of the house. While the journey to the cellar is short, it feels like it's a million miles away. I jump to every possible conclusion as I make my way towards it.

What if he fell down the stairs in a rush to take cover and knocked himself out?

What if he has no water and overheated down there?

What if he's down there with a woman? How will I explain that to my kids?

"Bryan!" I yell as I finally reach the shelter. "Bryan, are you in there?" I call, pounding on the metal door. My eyes dart to the house. Maybe he's inside. Maybe he's sleeping and this happened during the night. Maybe I'm freaking out for no reason.

That's when I hear his voice.

"Madi!" His voice sounds barely audible inside the shelter. "Madi, I think the door is stuck! My phone is dead and there's no service down here."

"Bryan!" I yell back, relieved. "Yes, you have a huge tree branch across the door. I can't move it." I say, trying anyway, hoping that adrenaline will help me. It doesn't budge.

"Call Andrew! He and Cody can come get it."

Before he even finishes talking, I pull the phone from my pocket and call Tyler.

"Hello?" she answers groggily.

"Hey. It's Madi. I'm at Bryan's. He is trapped in the storm shelter. There's a huge branch across the door. Can you send

Andrew to help? Have him bring Cody, too. This thing is massive."

"He'll be right there," Tyler says. "Hang tight."

* * *

"One... two.... three!" Andrew yells as he and Cody attempt to team lift the branch from the top of the shelter. Both men struggle, but in the end, the branch doesn't move.

"Damnit." Cody groans, stepping back from the branch. "Man, Bryan, when you try to do something you don't hold back, do you?" He laughs. "Bet you wish you had put the shelter ten feet to the left."

"Shut up." Bryan groans from inside the shelter.

"It's fine. We'll use my truck and pull it off." Andrew yells down to Bryan. "Hang tight."

"Not like I'm going anywhere, dumbass!" Bryan yells back with a chuckle.

I have to admit; I appreciate that he is at least finding some humor in this situation. If I were trapped in the ground, I'd be losing my mind by now. The thought of being in his shoes causes me to shudder. Who knows what bugs and other critters he is standing down there with?

Cody walks over to stand next to me while Andrew gets his truck. "What a freaking morning." He says with a laugh. "But, don't worry. We will get him out of there in no time."

"Hey, I'm just glad I found him. And equally glad that I'm not stuck down there with him." I admit.

"I'm surprised you were out here this morning to begin with. I thought you'd be at home watching kids."

I shrug. "Well, I should be. I ran out of coffee, so I went to Drip to get some more. Your mother-in-law told me she heard there were a bunch of trees down on the outside of town, so I thought I'd just drive by to see how his new place did. I wasn't planning to come down the driveway, but something told me to. I'm glad I did."

Cody nods. "I'm glad you did, too."

"Nathan's girlfriend is my part-time summer helper. She is at the house filling in for me. My neighbor, Carolyn, is over there helping, too. They can hold the fort down until I get there. I just want to stick around and make sure he is okay." I glance back at the girls. They are settled on the patio with my phone, watching a movie while we wait for Bryan to be freed. "Hopefully, this won't scar them too much." I say, nodding towards the kids.

"Nah." Cody says, waving me off. "Kids are resilient." He offers before making his way towards Andrew, who is attaching a ratchet strap to the back of his truck.

"That's what I hear." I call back to him as I make my way towards the girls. I take a seat next to them, leaning over slightly to see the movie they have queued up on my phone. Cinderella, Kate's most recent obsession. Not that I mind. It could certainly be worse.

I turn back to look at Cody and Andrew. The strap is hooked to the back of the truck and is now tied around the branch. Cody is standing by the branch to guide it, while Andrew slowly inches the truck forward. The limb that seemed so unmovable before now easily slides off the shelter and onto the ground nearby. Cody yells to Andrew that they are good, and then lifts the door to the shelter, freeing Bryan.

Bryan squints in the early morning sun as he climbs the steps from the shelter and his feet land on the grassy area. He turns to examine the limb. "Holy shit." He mutters, shaking his head. "It's no wonder I couldn't get out of there." He says, turning to address Andrew and Cody. "Thank you for your help." He says.

"It's nothing." Cody assures him. "That's what friends are for."

"And you." Bryan says, making his way towards me.

I'm standing at the edge of the patio now. As soon as he crawled out of the concrete box, I got up and then paused, with tears rolling down my face. Now I couldn't stop them if I tried.

"What were you doing out here this morning?" He asks, rushing towards me and wrapping his arms around my waist, lifting me from the ground. "I don't know how long I would have been stuck down there if it weren't for you." He admits. "Thank you."

I look down at him, as he still holds me in the air, and our lips crash into one another. "Bryan, I feel like such a jerk. I went to bed after we got done sheltering last night and forgot to text you to make sure you were good."

Bryan chuckles. "It's alright, Freckles. It'll take a hell of a lot more than a tree branch to take me out."

* * *

"What a day." I say, plopping down on the sofa after the last daycare kid leaves for the night. Even my daughters have already left with their father. "No matter how much coffee I've drank today, I am still dying for a nap."

"You could have taken one." Becca laughs from her seat on

228

the floor where she is sterilizing toys. "I could have handled things while you rested."

I smile softly. "You're so sweet. And yes, you would have done great with them. But, I could never relax with a house full of kids. Thank you for offering, though." I say with a laugh. "At least it's Friday and I can sleep in tomorrow. Maybe I'll sleep in all weekend." I admit, with a large yawn.

Becca stands up and studies the toys spread all around her. "I think that's everything." She declares with a satisfied grin.

"Thank you." I smile. "For everything. You really showed up for me today and I appreciate it so much." I pick up my phone and quickly calculate her earnings for the week. "Becca, I'm giving you a little extra for saving my ass this morning. I'm Cash Apping you now."

She laughs. "Thank you, but really, it was no problem. I was happy to help, and it was kind of exciting to see if I could manage things on my own." She admits. "Madi, you are such a great mentor. You have seriously taught me so much. I love working for you. I think I decided I want to go to school for my Early Childhood Degree."

A smile spreads across my face. "Oh Becca. I love that. The world can never have enough people that truly understand child development. Especially ones that are so good at it like you are. If that's what you decide to do, I'll do everything I can to help you along the way. Goodness knows Fawn Creek needs all the daycare options we can get."

"Thank you. That means a lot coming from you." She says, as she makes her way to the coat rack and swings her backpack over her shoulder. "I'll see you on Monday. Have a good weekend and I hope you get plenty of rest."

"I'm planning on it for sure." I say with a grin, just as my

229

phone chimes to alert me of a text.

Bryan: Kids all gone for the night?
Madison: Yep!
Bryan: I'm coming to pick you up. I have a surprise for you.

I stare down at the phone. Twenty-four hours ago I was checked out of this relationship. I was sure he was cheating and honestly, nothing has happened yet to convince me otherwise. If he hadn't been trapped in that damn storm shelter, I would probably still not be talking to him at all.

Instead, I'm dashing around my house, changing my clothes and touching up my makeup before he shows up to get me. But nothing has changed. He was still hiding something from me. He was still being mysterious. And I know that I'm not going to just move past that. I'm going to have to confront him. And if he can't show me exactly what he was hiding from me, then I guess we need to go our separate ways.

I lean over the bathroom sink and work to reapply my lip gloss and then finger comb the waves in my hair. I've already changed into a T-shirt and a pair of cutoff jean shorts. Satisfied with how I look, I step away from the mirror and make my way towards the living room, just as the doorbell rings.

I rush to the door and fling it open to find Bryan leaning against the door frame waiting for me. As soon as our eyes meet, he reaches out and wraps an arm around my waist, pulling me in close to him. He kisses me deeply and passionately as though it's been weeks, not hours, since the last time we touched.

He pulls back and leans his forehead against mine. "I've been waiting all day for that." He admits with a growl. "I hope you packed an overnight bag."

"I," I stutter. "I didn't... but I could."

"You should." He teases with a wink.

Without a pause, I turn and make my way back towards my bedroom to put together an overnight bag. As I work on filling the bag, I realize that, once again, I've already forgotten that I wanted to confront this man. I see him and the only thing I can think about is being wrapped in his arms, and even more so, in his bed sheets. I have to talk to him before any clothes come off. That has to be the deal. This can't go further until the air is clear.

I toss my weekender bag over my shoulder and make my way back towards the living room to find Bryan sitting on the couch waiting for me. When our eyes meet, he smiles warmly. "Hey, beautiful. Are you ready?"

I let out a sigh and drop the bag on the floor by my feet. "Just about. I need to talk to you first."

Bryan's smile fades. "About what? Is everything okay?"

I shake my head. "I don't know."

"What's wrong? Did I do something?" He asks, turning to face me and lifting my hand.

"Maybe." I admit with a shrug.

"What was it?" He furrows his brow. "I can't fix it if I don't know what I did wrong."

I pause, trying to think of how to continue this conversation without accusing him, but come up short. All I can do is just say what I'm thinking. I take a deep breath and dive in. "Bryan, who were you texting yesterday?"

"Texting? When?"

"When you were here helping with mud day. You were messaging someone named Carrie. But whenever I got anywhere near you, you would just hide your phone."

Bryan shakes his head. "No, Madi. It's not what you think."

"It sure doesn't look that way."

"What does it look like, then?" He challenges.

"Well, frankly, it looks like you are messing around with some lady named Carrie."

Bryan laughs. "That's... that's not what's going on."

"Then what is going on?" I demand, a little louder than intended. "Bryan, I'm sorry, but I've been cheated on already. I can't go through this again."

"I can't tell you." Bryan says. "But I can show you."

Chapter 28

"Okay, here we are." Bryan says, bringing his truck to a stop next to his shop. "Let's go."

I turn and look towards the beige metal building and scrunch my nose. "In there? What in there could possibly be what you were hiding?"

Bryan climbs out of the truck and turns to look at me. "Well, get out and I'll show you."

I let out a heavy breath and follow suit, climbing out of the truck and closing the door. I follow Bryan into the house and wait for him to turn on the lights. As the light comes on, I look around the dusty shop, honestly surprised by how much has changed since he moved in here. At one point, this place was full of nothing but dirt and cobwebs. Now the walls are lined with toolboxes, workbenches, and tables full of oil covered car parts. In the bay furthest from the door, is something covered in a dark blue tarp. Bryan motions his head towards it. "Come check this out." He says.

I follow in his footsteps as we approach the tarp.

"Are you ready for your surprise?" He asks with a gleam in his eyes.

"I.. guess so?"

With that, in one movement, he pulls the tarp away and

tosses it onto the floor in the space behind him. In front of us sits an old, rusty Volkswagen beetle.

I pause and study the machine. "I don't understand. What is this for?"

"For you, silly," He chuckles. "It's definitely not for me. I barely fit in the thing."

"You bought me a bug?" I ask, moving around the car to inspect it.

"Yeah," He says with a shrug, as if he's telling me he picked me up a snack from the gas station. "It doesn't run, of course, and it needs a shit ton of work. But I thought that maybe the two of us could work on it together. It might be a fun little project. If you're up for it. If not, I'll sell it and we can forget this whole thing ever happened."

A grin spreads across my face. "Yes, absolutely." I answer, before realizing that this may be more than I can do much with. "But restoring a car isn't cheap."

"You're right. It's not. But, we can do it as inexpensively as possible. We can visit junk yards on weekends, looking for parts, and you can save a lot of money on labor by paying me in... other ways." He adds with a wink.

"Like what? Helping with your laundry?"

"Sure, yeah, laundry." He teases. "I just know you said you loved bugs and wished you'd had one. So, I couldn't resist when I saw it on Facebook Marketplace. I picked it up yesterday after leaving your house."

I stand on tiptoe and kiss his lips. "Thank you. This is the coolest thing anyone has ever bought for me."

"You're welcome. And I'm sorry I had to be sneaky about it. Carrie is a lady from the next town over. She had it for sale on Facebook. Her husband bought it years ago, with full intentions of working on it, eventually. Unfortunately, he passed away last year, and she just wanted to get it out of her yard. She sold it to me for two hundred dollars. She was very excited to find out what I was planning to do with it. All she wants is some photos of it when we get done." As though he needs to prove his point, he holds up his phone to show me the conversation.

I don't even bother reading the text. The fact that I assumed the worst, when Bryan was just trying to do something nice for me makes me feel bad enough. Just because Ben hurt me, doesn't mean that Bryan would.

"We can do that. Hell, we can pick her up and take her for a drive if she wants."

"I bet she'd loved that." Bryan agrees. "So, does that mean you're done being mad at me?"

I nod sheepishly. "I'm sorry I doubted you. I know I should have asked first. After everything I went through with Ben, it has been hard for me to learn to trust again."

Bryan reaches over and pulls me close. "Freckles, you are stuck with me. I'm not going anywhere and the last thing I would do is try to chase after any other woman. You are everything I have ever wanted. The day I saw you, I knew exactly why I've never settled down with anyone before. My heart knew you were out there. I just had to wait for you to find me. I love you too much to throw away what we have."

"I love you, too." I confess, burying myself against him.

"Now that all of that is settled, let's go inside. I have steaks set aside for dinner and a new fire pit to break in afterwards. Plus another surprise for you."

I raise a brow. "Another one? Nothing could be better than this." I snuggle close to him and then look up at him. "And a fire? It's kind of warm outside for that, isn't it?"

He shrugs. "Kinda, but I have a tree limb that pissed me off this morning. It's time to show it who's boss."

I laugh. "In that case, I'm in. That tree will know never to mess with us again."

Bryan and I hop in the truck and make the drive to the house. Once inside, we turn on the light and I see exactly what surprise he was talking about.

"You built a shelf for my ugly cow painting?" I ask, making my way towards the painting that is now displayed on a shelf full of battery powered candles, right next to his massive TV.

"I told you I would find a prominent place for it." He says with a laugh.

I shake my head. "You have got to take that down and throw it away."

"No way. I told you. I'd never throw away a gift. The cow is here to stay."

* * *

"So, what you're saying is that you jumped to conclusions for no reason." Ava says, taking a seat on my porch swing, with a glass of wine in her hand. "That checks out."

I groan. "Yeah, that's about the gist of it."

Ava reaches over and squeezes my hand. "It's okay, friend. After what you went through with Ben, it's understandable that it's a little harder to trust someone. But you've got to remember that Ben and Bryan are not the same. Bryan is a good man, and he loves you with all his heart. I truly don't think he's the kind to play games the way Ben did."

"I don't think so either." I agree.

"And he bought you a car?" Ava shakes her head. "That's kind of a big commitment."

I let out a heavy sigh. "Well, in his defense. It wasn't an expensive car. He bought it for two hundred dollars."

"Yeah, and how long will it take the two of you to work on it? A year? Two years? You don't buy a project like that for a fling. A car restoration is a commitment. You're as good as married, my friend." She says, nudging me. "Might as well pick out colors. I mean, besides pink."

I grimace. "Slow down there, Ava. I am in no hurry to do that again."

But Ava isn't listening. "Damn, that means I'm going to have a new neighbor. I hope the next person isn't a jerk. But, I guess I will probably be your Realtor, so I could probably do some vetting..."

I shake my head. "Ava, stop spiraling. I'm not even engaged yet. And even if I was, who says I'm moving?"

"Well... he did just buy all that land and get a new house. How many bedrooms does he have? Enough for a family?"

I pause to think. "It's a four-bedroom, two-bathroom house."

"So, room for your girls and a new baby." Ava decides, wiggling her brows.

"Oh my gosh, Ava." I scoff. "I thought you were just coming over for a glass of wine and to swing on my porch. Now I'm married and pregnant? This escalated quickly."

"Sometimes it's just like that." Ava sips her wine and smiles softly. "I am glad it ended up to be nothing. You deserve to be happy and I think Bryan is the right one to make it happen."

I nod. "I think so, too."

Chapter 29

"Ladies and gentlemen, welcome to our annual Fawn Creek Founders' Day Celebration!" The voice of the mayor booms across the sound system in the city park. "Just a reminder that we have an impressive list of activities happening here today! At eleven o'clock sharp, we will host our much anticipated pie-eating contest. I don't know about you, but I can't wait to see if Jerry Burris, our reigning champ, can keep a hold of his title this year. But until then, be sure to visit our amazing craft and food vendors, try your arm at the dunk tank, or get some practice in for tonight's corn hole tournament. We still have room for a few more teams if you'd like to sign up. Whatever you choose to do, have fun!"

I make my way through the crowd, with Kate and Kenzi by my side towards Ava's real estate booth.

"Hey!" Ava smiles brightly. She's wearing a Fawn Creek Homes T-shirt in her signature color, a bright royal blue, with a pair of black shorts. Her long black hair is up in a ponytail.

"How do you look so beautiful when it's eight million degrees outside?" I groan. "And whose idea was it to have an all day festival during July in Kansas? I think I'm melting. I'm about to volunteer myself for the dunk tank so I can cool off."

Ava pauses to use her handheld fan. "I know, it's not ideal, but I make so many connections at these events, I can't turn down being here. Speaking of the dunk tank, I'm pretty sure your boyfriend is about to be in there. Derek is in there and then Bryan is right after him."

"Mom, can we go dunk Bryan? Please?" Kate asks excitedly.

"I thought you liked Bryan?" Ava asks, raising a brow.

"I do! He's really nice and funny. But I still think it would be fun to dunk him. Besides, he will probably be happy to get in the water." She adds.

I look across the park and look at Bryan. He's standing next to the dunk tank talking to Derek. Derek is wearing a dark grey Fawn Creek Police T-shirt and shorts, and he is looking a bit too dry himself.

"Sure. Let's go get him and maybe Derek too." I say with a shrug before turning back to Ava. "Do you need anything? Water? Food?"

Ava waves me off. "I'm good for now. My mom is on her way up here with Piper. I'll have her grab me some lunch from the macaroni and cheese food truck when she gets here."

My eyes dart around the park. "I didn't realize The Noodle Truck was coming today. No matter how hot it is, I'm always up for some macaroni and cheese."

"Same." Ava agrees.

"Mom, let's go!" Kate whines. "I don't want to miss my chance to take Uncle Derek down."

I let out a laugh. "Okay, girl. I didn't realize you were so competitive. Let's go."

* * *

239

"Sorry. Honestly, I don't know what got into Kate." I tell Bryan, trying to hold back my giggles as I hand him a beach towel. I watch as Kate, Kenzi and Piper make their way towards the playground equipment in the center of the park.

Bryan takes the towel from my hand and bends over to dry his hair. "It's fine. Honestly, with as hot as it is, the more time I can spend soaked in water, the better. She was doing me a favor."

"That kid has an arm like a rocket." Derek adds, as he joins us, dressed in dry clothes. "I think we've got a pro-softball player on our hands. Watching her play this summer was so much fun and it's just going to get better from there."

Bryan nudges me. "Are you ready to be a softball mom?"

I laugh. "Yes. Even though I truly don't understand a single thing about sports, I'll be the loudest one in the stands."

Bryan pulls me into a side hug and kisses the side of my head. "I'll be right there with you, Freckles." He promises me before turning to Derek. "Hey, how's Avery's boutique trailer doing? Is the air working?"

"It's as cold as ice in there." Derek reports. "I told her to charge admission for the other vendors to go inside and cool off."

"That'd probably make her a killing." I say with a laugh. "But Avery is too sweet to take advantage of people like that."

"MOM! Help!!" A loud scream sounds across the park, causing everyone to stop what they are doing to look around.

I'm the first one to spot Piper. She's at the top of the metal curly slide, frozen in place.

Ava quickly abandons her booth and runs across the park, making a beeline for the slide. "Piper!" She yells. "You've been up there a thousand times! Just slide down!"

"I can't!" Piper screams back. "There's a wasp on the slide! It's going to sting me!"

"Shit. Shit. Shit." Ava mutters to herself. "Okay, hang on. We will get you down! Just stay there." She promises, just as Eric, Carson's dad, makes his way towards us.

"What's going on?" He asks, looking from Ava to Piper.

Ava sighs. "There's a wasp on the slide. She's terrified of them after one stung her when she was three. She won't go down. I'm terrified of heights, but I can't just leave her up there."

"I've got it. Stay here." Eric promises, making his way up the slide, leaving Carson with me.

Before Ava can argue, Eric is halfway up the steps. He reaches the top of the landing and shouts back down to Ava. "It's just a mayfly!"

"PIPER!" Ava screams.

"It looked like a wasp!" Piper screams back in defense.

Eric slides down the metal slide, with Piper following close behind him. As Piper's feet hit the ground, Ava is waiting for them both at the bottom.

She turns to Eric. "Thank you. I feel like a fool right now. I guess Piper and I need some lessons about insects." She shakes her head.

Eric shrugs. "It's fine. For the record, Carson is terrified of mayflies, too."

"They are so creepy for no good reason." Carson says with a frown.

"And it's not even May. It's July. What are they even doing here?" Piper adds.

"Yes!" I agree. "They should only be able to show up in May. Just like June bugs. They shouldn't be out past their month, either."

"Exactly!" Piper squeals, before turning back to her group of friends. "Hey, the merry-go-round is empty! Let's get on it."

Kate's face lights up. "Bryan, will you spin us really fast?"

"Spin us until we PUKE!" Piper adds, excitedly.

Kenzi frowns and looks at Carson. "I don't want to puke."

He grimaces. "Yeah, me neither. Let's go play in the castle." He suggests, pointing to the wooden play set in the middle of the park with a castle-like tower in the center.

"Okay, I'll be the princess." Kenzi agrees as they run off.

I follow the kids, leaving Ava lost in conversation with Eric, finding a space between the play equipment and the merry-go-round so I can watch both girls.

It's not long before Avery is walking up to join me. "Hey! I call out to her. Did you abandon your post?" I tease her.

She shakes her head and looks back at her trailer. It's an old travel trailer that she and Derek worked all winter to fix up so she could use it as a mobile boutique for vendor events. "No, I needed to stretch my legs and use the restroom, so Derek took over for me."

I raise a brow. "Your camper doesn't have a bathroom?"

Avery laughs. "The toilet was the first thing to go. The last thing I'm going to do is spend my weekends emptying black water tanks that people decide to sneakily use while they are trying on clothes. Count me out." She scrunches her nose. "There are just some things I refuse to do."

"Faster!" Yells Kate, as the merry-go-round swirls in circles. The girl's faces are a complete blur.

"I'm doing my best!" Bryan says. "Don't forget I'm old."

"You're not that old. Go faster." Piper replies with a giggle.

"She did not inherit my anxiety." Ava says, joining us. "Lucky kid."

I elbow Ava gently. "You were talking to Eric for quite a while."

She waves me off. "Real estate stuff, nothing crazy. Speaking of. I'm going to head back to my booth now that the crisis is over. Can Piper hang out with you guys for a bit?"

"Of course. Go, build your empire. I've got Piper." I promise, as Bryan brings the merry-go-round to a stop.

"Okay, everyone, how about some snow cones? My treat." He offers, causing a gaggle of kids to erupt into shouts of excitement. At that, he points the kids toward the snow cone truck. Kenzi and Carson lead the way, followed by Kate and Piper.

"Your new dad is nice." Piper tells Kate. "Wait. Is he your new dad?"

"He's kind of like a dad." Kate shrugs. "Maybe he can be my other dad someday. It would be fun to have two. Race you to the snow cone truck!" She adds, taking off with Piper on her heels.

Fingers crossed, kid. Fingers crossed.

Chapter 30

Two Months Later

"How much longer until we get there?" Kate asks from the backseat.

I look at my daughter and wince. For some reason, my tiny baby suddenly looks like she's on the verge of being a preteen. The pair of purple fuzzy headphones draped around her neck certainly aren't helping matters much. She's growing up too fast.

"Nine hours and twenty minutes." I reply.

"That's forever!" Kate groans in response.

"Maybe you should take a nap. It'll make time go faster. Besides, that's why we got up so early, so you guys could get into the car and go back to sleep."

"I don't take naps anymore, Mom. I'm not a baby." Kate reminds me.

"Yeah, me neither." Kenzi adds.

I let out a sigh and shake my head. "Whatever you girls say. But it's still going to be a long drive, so you might as well get comfy."

"I'm just so excited to get to the beach!" Kenzi squeals. "Do you think we will see dolphins? And maybe a whale? Or a mermaid?"

"Mermaids don't exist, Kenzi." Kate hisses at her sister. "That's only stuff that babies believe in."

"Yeah, they do!" Kenzi argues. "Mom, mermaids are real, right?"

"Uh..." I pause, trying to buy myself some time. I hate lying to kids about things like this. But I also want them to be innocent for as long as possible. Innocence sure doesn't last as long as it used to.

"What do you think, Kenzi?" Bryan asks.

"I think they are real." She declares.

"Then that's all that matters," Bryan answers. "We probably won't see a whale, or a mermaid, since we will only be in the gulf of Mexico, but we might see some dolphins. Especially on the ferry."

"What's a ferry?" Kate asks.

"It's a giant boat that you drive your car onto and they float you across the water from one island to another. Our beach house is on a different island, so we will float over there and then go to our vacation place."

"And we might see dolphins? Really?" Kate asks.

"Maybe." Bryan shrugs. "There's no guarantee, but it's possible. I've seen them there before."

"Really? Dolphins in Galveston?" I ask, raising a brow.

"I wouldn't believe it myself if I hadn't seen it with my own eyes." Bryan confesses. "I've seen them on cruises leaving Galveston and on the ferry to Bolivar Island."

"Weird. I had no idea." I say, shaking my head, looking out the window before turning back to look at him. "Bryan, thanks again for taking the girls and I on a trip. It's been a long year and being able to take them to the beach means a lot to me. I could have never driven them through Houston on my own."

"I would have lost my mind worrying about you driving them to Galveston without me," Bryan admits. "Besides, I like Galveston. This will be a good break for all of us. The kids deserve a decent vacation before heading back into the school year."

"Don't forget about yourself." I add. "You have been so busy with your shop and then add dealing with us into the mix. That's a full-time job on its own."

Bryan reaches over and squeezes my hand. "It's a full-time job that I love. Life is so good now that I'm back home and settled in, so much better than I ever imagined. I feel just now is when my life is truly beginning."

"Beginning? You've done a lot of living already."

Bryan shakes his head. "No, I've done a lot of things. I've seen a lot of places, but I don't feel like I've really lived. This life." He says, lifting a hand off the steering wheel to motion around the car. "This is what I have been missing. The consistency of running my business. Having my mom and sister and niece nearby where I can see them more than once a year. And don't even get me started on you guys." He blushes. "You three are everything that I could have ever dreamed of for a family. I love our time together and doing life with you."

I reach over and grab his hand, that's now resting on his thigh. I squeeze it tightly. "We love doing life with you, too."

* * *

"Where are we?" Kenzi asks groggily from the middle seat of my minivan, interrupting the silence that Bryan and I have been driving in for over an hour now. The only sound has been

246

the quiet of the radio and Kenzi's gentle snoring.

"Hi, baby. Good timing." I reply, turning my face towards hers. "We are just getting ready to go over the bridge into Galveston. If you watch out your window, you'll be able to see the water here pretty soon."

"Does that mean we can play at the beach now?"

"Almost." Bryan assures her. "We are going to take the ferry to the island and then we will be at the beach house."

"Are we to the ferry yet?" Kate mumbles, still half asleep.

"Almost there." I reply. "Hey, what happened? I thought you were too big to take a nap?"

Kate groans in response. "I couldn't help it! We've been in the car forever."

"For a hundred thousand million hours." Kenzi adds.

"It has felt like that for sure." I reply with a laugh. "Do we need to find a place to stretch and potty before we make our way across town?"

"Actually, let's stop at the grocery store." Bryan suggests. "We can grab all the cold stuff we need for the weekend and save us a trip to the store later."

"Good plan. I'll map it for you." I say, pulling up my phone and quickly typing away. "Oh, wow."

"What?" He asks, turning to me with a puzzled look on his face.

I lower my voice to ensure the girls don't hear me. "Apparently, one of the grocery stores in Galveston is haunted."

Bryan snickers. "Okay. You don't honestly believe in that kind of stuff, do you?"

I shrug. "Yeah, I kind of do. I don't really have a reason not to." I continue scrolling around on my phone. "There are actually a lot of those things around here. If we didn't have the girls, I'd suggest we go on a ghost tour."

"Maybe next time." Bryan says with a wink, kissing the top of my hand. "If you like that kind of stuff, we need to visit Savannah one day, too. That place is very haunted."

Within the hour, we've gathered our groceries and made our way onto the ferry. As soon as the ferry takes off, Bryan motions for the girls to unbuckle.

"Okay guys, let's go," Bryan says, opening his car door. I follow suit, and move to the side of the van to let Kenzi out. Bryan helps Kate climb out of the van as well.

Together, the four of us walk to the side of the vessel to watch the water.

"Okay, this is actually really cool," Kate says, as she stares out into the water. "I hope we really do see a dolphin."

"While we wait, let's get a picture of the three of you together." Bryan decides, pulling his phone from his pocket.

Kate, Kenzi and I snuggle in close and turn to face Bryan with the water in the background. "Cheese!" We say in unison.

Bryan snaps the photo and then shows me the finished product to get my approval.

"That's perfect." I say, before leaning towards him to kiss his cheek, as the girls turn around and face the water in search of dolphins. "Thank you."

"Eh, it's easy to get a good photo when you have beautiful subjects." He answers with a wink.

I shake my head. "Not just for the photo. For all of this. For loving me and my kids despite my baggage."

"Baby, I'll carry your baggage anywhere." He smiles. "I love you and the girls. I'm sorry about the crap you've been through, but even if it takes me the rest of my life, I'm going to show you how special you are and love you the way you deserve to be loved."

"I love you, too." I say, leaning my head into him.

"I see one!" Kate yells, interrupting the tender moment. "Mom! Bryan! Is that a dolphin?"

I look up just in time to see a fin floating on top of the water, about fifty yards away from the ferry. Immediately, two more fins appear.

"That's a dolphin and her friends." Bryan confirms. "See the others?" He asks, as the dolphins circle along the top and back under the water.

"This is the coolest thing ever!" Kenzi squeals. She focuses on the dolphin friends swimming in the water. "Thank you, Bryan, for taking us to see them!" She wraps her arms around Bryan, still not removing her eyes from the gulf.

"You're welcome." He grins. "They're really cool, aren't they?"

"This is the best day of my life." Kate says, still not removing her eyes from the water.

"Even though you had to ride in the car for ten hours?" I ask, raising a brow.

"Yes." she confirms. "I would ride in the car for one hundred hours if it meant that I could see dolphins like this." Kate wipes at the corner of her eye.

I bend down to look at my daughter. "Kate, are you okay?" My eyes darting back and forth to look at the tears brewing in hers.

She nods. "Yeah. I'm just so happy." She confesses before reaching out to hug me.

"Oh, sweet girl." I say, kissing the top of her head.

I think it's safe to say that Bryan has officially won over my girls. And of course, he's won me over too.

* * *

"Okay girls. It's time to get ready for dinner!" I call out to Kate and Kenzi as they work diligently on their sandcastle.

"Mom, please, just ten more minutes?" Kate begs. "We are almost done!"

I eye the castle over the top of the book I'm reading. I have to admit, the columns they've constructed, and the moat filled with water, are quite impressive. Not to mention the shells they've used to decorate the entire exterior. "Okay, ten more minutes, but then we need to eat dinner. I'm ready for a shower."

Bryan looks up at me from his seat in the sand next to Kate. "Hey, why don't you go take your shower and then come get us when you're ready?"

I look down at my sand covered legs. "Are you sure? I don't want you to have to be in charge of the girls."

"Positive." Bryan nods. "Go. Take your time. We aren't quite done with our sandcastle and don't want to rush if we don't have to. Besides, you haven't had a minute to yourself this entire trip. Go relax. If we are done before you are, we will head in and start dinner."

"Okay." I agree, standing and dusting myself off the best I can. "I'll be back in just a little bit."

"Take your time." He repeats with a grin.

Twenty minutes later, I am slipping on a dark green cotton dress over my body, letting my freshly blow dried hair fall all around my shoulders. Bryan was right. I hadn't had a moment of quiet yet all day. The girls woke up before we did and climbed into our bed, immediately begging for food and for a walk on the beach. Ever since I first opened my eyes, we have been on the go.

I warned Bryan last night that this would be the case. Vacationing with kids isn't really a vacation. It's parenting in a foreign land. At least the looks on their faces when we got to the beach made the whole thing worth it.

I step out of the bathroom, expecting to find the three of them waiting for me in the living room, but a quick glance out the patio window confirms they are still in construction mode.

Carefully, I make my way down the stairs and towards my boyfriend and my children. Kenzi spots me first.

"Here comes Mommy!" She announces. "Mommy, come here! Look!"

I finish my journey towards them, to find the three of them standing in front of something scrawled in the sand, but I can't quite make out what it is.

"What did you make this time?" I ask, stretching my neck to get a peek.

"Come see for yourself." Bryan offers with a grin, holding out a hand towards me.

I close the distance between us and tilt my head. I let my eyes focus and then have to read it once more to make sure I'm not seeing things.

Will you marry me?

I look up from the writing to find Bryan, now on one knee next to me. He's holding up a dainty diamond ring in one hand and has a huge grin across his face.

"Say yes!" Kate pipes up. "Please, mommy."

"Pleaaase." Echos Kenzi.

I look from one of my girls to the other, and then let my eyes land on Bryan.

"Well, what do you say?" Bryan asks.

"Yes. Of course, yes." I tell him with a teary-eyed grin. "Yes, I'll marry you."

"Yay!" both of the girls call out, running sudden circles around us both.

"Can I be the flower girl?" Kate asks excitedly.

"No, I want to be the flower girl. I'm littler." Kenzi argues.

"I'm more mature, Kenzi." Kate argues.

"There can be more than one flower girl." I advise them, interrupting their argument, as I turn to Bryan, moving myself into his arms. "Are you sure you want to do this?" I joke. "We've been engaged for four seconds and it's already so full of drama."

"The three of you are worth every bit of drama."

Epilogue

The sound of the ringing church bells can surely be heard all across Fawn Creek as Bryan and I make our way out of the Methodist church, surrounded by our friends and family. The doors to the building fling open and outside everyone we love is flanking the sidewalk, waiting for our grand send off.

"Now!" I hear someone shout as all the wedding guests blow bubbles into the air, creating a beautiful backdrop for us to get away under.

I pause briefly to hug my daughters.

"You look beautiful, Mommy." Kate says with a wide smile.

"I'm going to miss you." Kenzi adds.

"I'm going to miss the both of you so much. But I'll be home in just a few days. You're going to have a great time with your dad while I'm gone."

I hug the girls once more and tell them goodbye before turning back towards Bryan.

"You ready, my beautiful wife?"

A giant smile spreads across my face. "So ready." I confirm, slipping my hand into his. "Let's go."

Bryan and I quickly make our way across the parking lot and into the getaway car, our baby pink Volkswagen beetle.

"They sure did a number on this thing, didn't they?" I

laugh, admiring the tin cans tied to the bumper and the words proclaiming "Just Married!" across the back windshield.

"Yeah, they did." Bryan grumbles. "I'm going to get us down the street and then I'm pulling over to cut off those cans. We put way too much work into this thing for a can to ricochet off the road and scratch the new paint job."

"Agreed." I say with a laugh, before turning back once more to look at our friends and family. They are all still standing on the sidewalk of the church, watching and waiting for us to drive away. I wave and turn back to Bryan, kissing his lips once more before we make our getaway as husband and wife.

Bonus Content – A Sneak Peek at Ava's Story: Signed, Sealed, Delivered.

"Piper, it's time to get up!" I say as I lean into her bedroom doorway. "You've gotta get ready for the first day of school."

Piper's eyes snap open at the mention of school, and she jumps out of her bed.

"First grade! Yay!" she squeals as her feet land on the floor and she dashes towards the outfit we set out last night.

"Get dressed and then come down for breakfast. I'll drive you to school today for your first day, and then tomorrow you can start going to school in the morning with Kate."

"Okay. Don't forget to pack my lunch in my new Minecraft lunchbox!" Piper calls out to me as I leave her room and make my way down the stairs to the kitchen.

I warm up a frozen waffle and place a few strawberries on her breakfast plate. By the time her breakfast is ready and lunch is packed, Piper is already bounding down the stairs, dressed and ready.

"Can I have whipped cream and sprinkles on my waffle? And chocolate syrup?" Piper requests as she makes her way into the kitchen and takes a seat at the kitchen table.

"Isn't that kind of a lot of sugar for the first day of school?" I ask with a raised brow.

"It's the same as a donut," Piper argues. "Grandma told me

255

so."

"You have a point." I shrug as I make my way towards the fridge to get the can of whipped cream. "But this isn't an everyday thing. Just a first day of school thing. Deal?"

"Deal."

I dress Piper's waffle and slide the plate in front of her. Then, I make my way to my leather tote bag that's sitting on the kitchen counter. I pull out my planner and open it to check my agenda for the day.

As soon as I see the date, my stomach flips, and just for a second the numbers on the page blur. *August 18th.* Today isn't just any date. On this date seven years ago, Piper's dad passed away. One minute I was just starting a typical morning, and the next, the chief of police for Fawn Creek was knocking on my door to tell me that Zach was gone.

Every year, I assume this date will be easier, and every year I find out that I'm wrong.

"Mom. Mom. Mommy... you okay?" Piper asks, finally breaking through my thoughts.

I look down at my sweet little blonde-haired girl. "Yes, sorry. I was just thinking."

"About what?"

I shake my head. "Just things I need to do today," I lie.

I can't tell Piper that today is the anniversary of her dad's death. She's too excited. I can't make her sad. Not today.

* * *

We make our way across the grassy lawn in front of Fawn Creek Elementary when Piper spots her best friend, Kate, and her little sister, Kenzi. They are crossing the street, holding hands with their mom, Madison.

"Hey," I say to Madison, closing the distance towards them. "Kenzi, do you get to start school today, too?"

Kenzi nods excitedly while wearing a hot pink kitty cat backpack that's bigger than she is.

"Yes! I get to go to school with my sister now! And Piper. But I don't get to eat lunch here," she pouts.

I nod. "I get it. It stinks that preschool is only a half day, but at least your mom makes good lunches, and you'll get to take a nap at home instead of at school."

"I guess," she replies.

I turn to Kate. "What about you? Are you excited to start first grade?"

"Yes!" Kate squeals. "And I'm so happy Piper's in my class. Maybe the teacher will let us sit by each other."

"Maybe so," I say as my eyes wander across the lawn, landing on a face that I haven't seen in years, not since Zach's funeral.

It's Zach's sister, Emilee. Our eyes meet, and she sends me a half smile.

Last I knew, she lived in Missouri, but apparently she's back and dropping off her own kid for school today. A cousin that Piper barely knows. If Zach were still here, Piper would know her cousin well. But life had its own plans.

I want to go to her and ask when she moved home, but our relationship just hasn't been the same since he died. Ever since then, I've had a feeling that Emilee blames me for his being gone.

In all honesty, I blame myself, too.

"Bye, Mom. We're going in." Piper snaps me back to reality.

"Wait. Don't you want me to walk you in?" I ask, stopping the girls mid-stride as they head towards the front door.

Piper shakes her head. "Nope. We are big kids now. We can go in on our own."

I frown and bend down to give her a hug and kiss the top of her head.

"Okay, if you insist. Have a good day. I'll pick you up after school today. I love you."

"Love you, too!" Piper calls over her shoulder as she, Kate, and Kenzi make their way towards the open front doors of the building.

I watch them disappear, almost unable to believe how grown up she looks.

As the girls disappear inside, I turn to look back at Emilee, thinking that maybe I can still catch her. But she's already gone.

"Well, I guess I'll get back home and wait for my non-school kids to get there." Madison interrupts my train of thought and brings me back to reality. "Have a good day, Ava!"

"You too," I reply with a wave as we part ways towards our cars.

I'm still not sure how I can have a good day at this rate.

But who am I kidding? *August 18th is never a good day.*

About the Author

Michelle Lynn Ross is a self professed hopeless romantic from Southeast Kansas. When she isn't writing, she enjoys traveling, reading and spending time with her husband and three daughters. She also has been known to waste too much time on social media when she should be working on her next book. Should not be left alone with chips and queso.

You can connect with me on:
🌐 https://michellelynnross.com
📘 https://www.facebook.com/ThatsWhatShellSaid

Subscribe to my newsletter:
✉ https://substack.com/@michellelynnross

Also by Michelle Lynn Ross

There's No Place Like Home

Book One of the Fawn Creek Series

When Tyler Burris's long-term relationship falls apart, she's forced to return to her small hometown of Fawn Creek, Kansas—a place she swore she'd never live again. Her plan? Regroup, then get out fast. But between a rogue rooster, nosy neighbors, and a surprisingly charming (and grumpy) next-door neighbor, Tyler might just discover that what she's been searching for has been waiting for her all along.

Small Town Famous

Book Two of the Fawn Creek Series

After escaping a toxic relationship, Avery Thompson is focused on rebuilding her life and raising her daughter—solo. But when a new side hustle as a content creator brings unexpected attention (and chaos), she starts to find her spark again. Add in a swoony local cop who sees past her scars, and Avery must decide if she's ready to risk her heart... or let fear hold her back.